# THE NANNY WHO
# KISSED HER BOSS

# THE NANNY WHO KISSED HER BOSS

BY

BARBARA McMAHON

MILLS
BOON

First published in Great Britain 2012
by Mills & Boon, an imprint of Harlequin (UK) Limited.
Large Print edition 2012
Harlequin (UK) Limited, Eton House,
18-24 Paradise Road, Richmond, Surrey TW9 1SR

© Barbara McMahon 2012

ISBN: 978 0 263 22611 9

Harlequin (UK) policy is to use papers that are natural, renewable and recyclable products and made from wood grown in sustainable forests. The logging and manufacturing process conform to the legal environmental regulations of the country of origin.

Printed and bound in Great Britain
by CPI Antony Rowe, Chippenham, Wiltshire

# CHAPTER ONE

SAVANNAH Williams rolled over on her right side and pulled the covers over her head. It was morning, she could tell by the bright sunlight flooding her bedroom. But she was not ready to get up. She'd arrived home late last night after the airplane trip from hell. It had routed her all over the United States and got her to New York long after midnight when she'd been up before dawn on the west coast to make that first flight.

The apartment was quiet. Her sister was on assignment. She relaxed and tried to fall back asleep. Why hadn't she put a blackout shade on the window? She just wanted a few more hours of rest.

The ring of the phone jarred.

"Oh, for heaven's sake!" She threw back the sheet and stalked to the living room where the apartment phone was ringing. She'd turned off her cell, so naturally this phone had to ring.

"It better be good," she snapped into the receiver when she snatched it up.

"Good morning, Savannah. It's Stephanie. Did you have a good trip?" The cheerful voice was not what Savannah wanted to hear this early.

"The cruise was okay except it snowed two days. So much for lying on the deck while the children napped. And the two darling dears of Dr. and Mrs. Lightower were not the angels the parents purported them to be. I was never so thankful to end an assignment. Talk about spoiled brats! The flight home—or should I say the *flights* home—were horrible. I was routed from Alaska to LA to Dallas then Chicago, then I swear I thought I was going to be sent through Atlanta, but fortunately bad weather kept that airport off the schedule, so I got sent to Boston before ending up in New York at two o'clock in the morning!" She was practically yelling the last, but only heard Stephanie's giggles in the background. So much for sympathy.

"I was trying to sleep in," she grumbled.

"Oh, poor you. Go back to sleep in a minute. You have a new assignment and the client actually postponed his trip to make sure it coincided with your availability. This one's right up your alley—one child, a teenager. Parents are divorced, mother has custody. However, the teen is with her father now and will be for the summer apparently. Could be a bonding experience for them, I suppose."

"What could?" Savannah asked. She was growing wider awake the longer Stephanie kept her on the phone. For what? She was off the clock and wanted to catch up on sleep and fun before taking another assignment from Vacation Nannies.

"Backpacking in the High Sierras," Stephanie said.

Savannah stared out the window to the sliver of a view of the Hudson River she and her sister enjoyed from their apartment. Glass and concrete and that tiny sliver compared to endless vistas of mountain ranges? Clear blue sky instead of the heavy layer of smog over New York?

But backpacking?

"How come Stacey gets to lounge around at the beach on the Med and I'm stuck lugging a heavy backpack on a trail where there won't even be hot and cold running water?"

"Luck of the draw. Plus you're our resident expert on troublesome teens."

"Oh, joy, another challenge. When do we meet?" she asked. Rule number one of Vacation Nannies was that both parties had to agree to the assignment. Which usually worked to make sure the match between nanny and children was harmonious, but she had seriously been off with the Lightower children. Who expected them to behave so nicely at the initial meeting and then turn into terrors? Not that she hadn't been able to cope, but the carefree cruise she'd anticipated had not been the case.

"Friday. If everything goes okay, you'll depart next week and be gone three weeks."

"How old's the teen?" Savannah had specialized in adolescent behavior when getting her degree in education. She had a special bond for children who had reached the whacked-out stage of teenagedom, which included recalcitrant and defiant behavior.

"She's fourteen. Lives here in New York."

Savannah could hear papers being turned over, Stephanie was obviously referring to interview notes. She plopped down on the sofa, giving up any thought of going back to sleep until later. "Never mind giving me all the info. I'll be by later to look at the file. Anything else I should know?"

"Do you have hiking boots?"

"Of course, remember my trip to the Adirondacks last fall? It was a glorious week tramping round the forest and enjoying at all the colorful foliage. The pair I got then are well worn in. How cold is it in the High Sierras in June?"

"Check the national weather outlook. I'll con- firm you'll be there on Friday at eleven. Oh, and, Savannah…" Stephanie sounded hesitant.

Savannah sat up at her tone.

"What?"

"The dad is Declan Murdock."

Savannah frowned, almost hearing Stephanie holding her breath after delivering that bomb- shell.

"I'm not going," she said. *Declan Murdock.* It had been seven years since she'd seen him. Seven lonely years of trying to forget the man she'd loved with all the fresh bright hope of first love—and who had dumped her so unceremo- niously.

"He asked especially for you."

"That's hard to believe." And was like a knife twisting in her. He'd left her because of Jacey. Now he wanted her to watch her while he was off doing what—oh yeah, backpacking. What had happened to Jacey's mother? They were divorced—again?

"Why backpacking in the mountains? Why isn't he just sticking around New York while he has Jacey? They could see shows, visit museums, go to the shore. Bond in New York."

"I don't inquire as to why our clients do things. Friday morning at his office. I think you know where." Stephanie hung up before Savannah could utter another word.

She slammed down the phone. "For this I had to get up early?"

Declan Murdock. She hadn't seen him in years, hadn't thought about him in—well, at least maybe one year. She wished she could say she'd forgotten him as fast as he'd probably forgotten her. But she'd been incredibly hurt by their parting. She'd been dreaming of a wedding and he'd been lured back to his ex-wife because of a daughter he hadn't known existed.

For the longest time she'd gone over everything, replaying in her mind every word he'd uttered at that final meeting, trying to see where things could have gone differently.

"Water long under the bridge," she muttered, going to get coffee to jump-start her brain. Did Stephanie really think she'd take the job? Be alone with Declan and his daughter for three weeks?

"Why not ask me to plunge a knife into my heart to begin with. It would be just as painful," she mumbled, watching the coffeemaker drizzle the brew into the carafe. Divorced, Stephanie had said. So when had that happened? What about Declan's determination to make a go of his marriage for the sake of a daughter he'd just discovered?

No one would blame her for turning down a request for an assignment from the man who had broken her heart. The man against whom she had judged all other men ever since—and had usually found them lacking.

Maybe she should have asked the Lightowers to extend her services—even the horrible brats looked better than facing Declan again.

Taking her coffee, she went back to the sofa and gazed out the window. She wondered if he'd aged much. She'd learned how successful his sporting goods chain had become. Everything he touched seemed golden.

Divorced. Her curiosity got the better of her. Dare she risk her peace of mind by seeing him again? Any feelings she'd had for him seven years ago had evaporated. She'd become much more wary, much more cynical about men's intentions.

And how could she watch his daughter—the reason he'd left her. She'd been so in love, and she'd thought he had, as well. How could he so easily have tossed that love aside to marry Margo—or rather to remarry her when she'd shown up years after their divorce saying Declan was a father. He'd had the paternity tests done and had then been convinced he needed to marry Jacey's mother again and build a strong family unit.

Forget about the college student who had adored him. Forget about the plans and dreams they'd had. Once he'd uttered the fateful words, Savannah had wished him well and left the coffee shop, tears not falling until she was home.

So what had happened to his precious plans that had brought him full circle back into her life?

Curiosity won. She'd go to the interview. It wouldn't go well, she already knew that. But the reputation of Vacation Nannies was on the line. She didn't want him bad-mouthing the company because of personal feelings. Feelings that should have died seven years ago.

"That *did* die seven years ago!" she repeated aloud. "I'm so over you, Declan Murdock."

Friday, Savannah dressed with care. She was no longer the college student dating an up-and-coming businessman. She went with the most trendy outfit she had, and spiked her short hair the way she liked it. Her outfit was the fourth she'd tried on this morning, wanting to get just the right look of successful businesswoman and capable nanny. The navy slacks, white blouse and sassy scarf declared her achievement.

He'd done well, she'd learned a couple of years ago. Well, so had she and her sister. Maybe not on the scale he'd reached, but wildly prosperous. She and Stacey had planned their business long before they were able to start it. The one course she especially wanted to take in her senior year in college was Start-ups on a Shoestring—taught by visiting guest lecturer Declan Murdock shortly after he began his sporting goods company. She'd hung on his every word. First for what she could learn about business, then for what she could learn about the man himself. When he'd asked her out, she'd gone. There were rules at the college against faculty dating students but as a guest lecturer, he wasn't really faculty.

Only a few years older than she, he'd captured her imagination and fired her enthusiasm about her business model for Vacation Nannies. Before long the business talk had turned personal and by Christmas that year she'd fallen in love. She remembered their talk about surfing together off the coast of Maine, the fun she'd had slugging a softball out of the park to his wild cheering, the thrill of roller-blading in Central Park together. Visiting museums and art galleries when the weather was bad, lost in a world of two despite the crowded places.

She shook off the memories. She was an accomplished businesswoman in her own right. She would see him, refuse the job and that would be that.

She gave the cabdriver the address. Savannah knew exactly where the company headquarters was for Murdock Sports. She'd met him there many evenings, to give them more time together. She didn't want to remember, but ever since Stephanie's call the memories had flooded in.

At least she had the teensy consolation that she wasn't still some lovestruck idiot pining for a man who'd married a woman he didn't love for the sake of a daughter who had been kept from him the first seven years of her life.

Maybe he'd say or do something so outlandish at the interview she could instantly say no. Highly unlikely, but she lived in hope. Truth was, she could turn down the assignment for no reason at all. She didn't answer to him.

But Vacation Nannies thrived on referrals. He probably moved in such rarified air these days he could give their company a big boost.

Three weeks was a mere twenty-one days. She could do anything for a short time.

The first thing Savannah noticed when she stepped into the building was the major renovations since she'd last been there. The reception area was larger and very upscale. Most suitable to the image of a very successful company. *Let the public believe you're highly successful, and you'll be highly successful,* had been one of his axioms. So his business instincts had been right on. He was a huge success. Despite her heartbreak, she'd picked up some information over the years from the local business news. If nothing else, she'd learned solid business techniques and how to focus on the main goal from Declan's class.

Add the fact that the address of Vacation Nannies made a major impression on clients, also thanks to Declan. Granted she sometimes thought they paid way too much for the tiny offices they had, but the clientele they drew demanded the very best.

Savannah gave her name to the receptionist and was asked to wait. No hardship since she'd put off the interview entirely if she could. But there was no other nanny as suitable from their company so Stephanie had explained to her when she'd showed up at the office to read the file before the interview. The most important thing was to keep up the reputation of Vacation Nannies.

The concept—provide short-term, temporary nannies to watch children while the family was on vacation—had proven surprisingly popular. Savannah and Stacey had begun the business because of their own desire to travel and see the world. With the little money they had that would be unlikely. So they'd found a way to travel on someone else's dime.

After a degree in education, plus some business courses at NYU, Savannah had been instrumental in getting the business going. Soon there were more requests than she and Stacey could handle, so Stephanie had been hired to handle the scheduling aspect. Other nannies, trained at the prestigious Miss Pritchard's School for Nannies, were carefully vetted and hired. Now they had a dozen others on the payroll, and during the summer months everyone was fully booked.

To ensure the nannies weren't stuck for weeks with horrendous children or parents, the interview aspect went both ways. Either the prospective client could decline after meeting the nanny or the nanny could refuse to take the assignment.

So far there had only been a handful of refusals. She winced, thinking she'd make this another one.

She grew more nervous the longer she waited. What was she doing coming here? She didn't want to spend three weeks with Declan. Or with his daughter.

"Mr. Murdock can see you now," the receptionist said, rising and heading for the hall on the left. Her sleek toned looks gave mute testimony to the healthy lifestyle a sports aficionado could expect—especially if they used Murdock equipment.

Savannah wished she could have checked her makeup and hair one more time. It would never do not to be immaculately turned out and polished-looking. She hoped Declan didn't remember the casual clothes she'd worn in college. Money had always been tight in her family. After the first six months with their new venture, however, that had changed. Now she and her sister enjoyed high-end fashionable clothing, makeup and a professional hair stylist. No more letting her hair grow long like Stacey. Savannah liked it short and spiky. And the kids usually liked it, too. It was easy to care for. And if she were in the sun for long, the blond bleached out to almost white. Which was always a startling contrast to her tanned skin.

The receptionist handed her off to a personal assistant who took her to Declan's office—still located in the back corner of the warehouse-converted-to-offices. But the extremely modern look of chrome, leather and fine woods was a huge step up from when she'd visited before. His business model had obviously propelled his own firm into the stratosphere.

"Savannah," he said when the PA opened the door to usher her in. He stood behind the desk, studying her as she stepped into the office.

Savannah felt a catch in her breath. He looked the same. She'd forgotten how tall he was. While she was only five foot four when she stretched, Declan had to be close to six feet. Muscular and fit, he didn't look a day older than when she'd last seen him. His hair was still dark, not a strand of gray could she find. His eyes were a rich chocolate-brown, focused on her now. She could have stared back forever. For a moment she felt as tongue-tied as that college student who had been so in love. She nodded slightly, clinging to her composure with all she had. Wishing he'd aged, grown a pot belly and lost his hair.

"Hello, Declan." Yippee, her voice hadn't cracked. She hadn't stuttered or slapped his face. She also hadn't expected the jolt of awareness that spiked through her. Taking a slow breath she tried to relax, to treat him like any other prospective client. She wished she could forget the past that seemed to spring to the forefront. Why did long-dormant emotions have to blossom now?

"Connie, coffee for us both." He said to his PA, then looked at Savannah with an eyebrow raised in silent question.

"Thank you, that would be nice." They both had shared a love of strong coffee. Their final meeting had been at a coffee shop. She'd often wondered if he'd done that deliberately to make sure she didn't cause a scene in public.

"Thanks for coming. This is a bit awkward."

"You need a professional nanny for a trip you're taking. That's what our company specializes in. The past is dead, Declan."

He sat after she did and glanced away. Was he remembering their time together, their last meeting? She hoped he found this meeting *extremely* awkward. She would do nothing to ease the situation. After a long moment, she broke the silence.

"Do you still guest-lecture?" she asked.

He shook his head. "No time now. The business grew faster than I expected. The spring class that year was the last one I did. We've expanded to major markets around the country—which is the reason for the trip. I'm exploring the possibility of opening boutique stores in some resorts. So I'm combining business with pleasure. I want to spend a day or two at the San Francisco facility. It's fairly new. Then on to the mountains to test some new equipment. Then to one of the resorts in California that wants to discuss opening a boutique outlet there, offering only the sporting goods suitable for their resort."

She listened, but kept her expression impassive. So he was doing well, good for him. She was here merely to talk about the proposed trip.

He waited a moment and then cleared his throat. Was he as nervous as she felt? She hoped so. And hoped he rued the day he'd dumped her for Margo—daughter or not.

"I hear your company's doing well."

She nodded.

"I don't think I'd have pegged a firm like yours as a contender for growth, which shows how wrong I'd have been. I have friends who had one of your nannies for their trip to South America last year, the Spencers?"

"I think Stacey had that assignment. They visited Machu Picchu," Savannah said.

"Right. They highly recommend the agency to anyone who listens. And as many of us who socialize together have children, we all listened."

Connie brought in a tray with a carafe of coffee, sugar and cream and two mugs.

"Thanks," Declan said. She nodded, smiled at Savannah and left, closing the door behind her.

Once they both had their coffee, Declan leaned back and studied her for a moment. "So tell me how this works."

"Stephanie didn't explain?" Savannah asked. Usually the prospective client got the complete rundown. Fees, limitations, expectations—the works.

"Mainly what I took away from meeting her was we both have to suit each other. I know you'd suit, what do you want to know about Jacey?"

"I need to meet your daughter," Savannah said.

He'd been divorced when she'd known him before. Now according to the interview at the office, he was divorced again. What had happened to that second go-round of marriage? Had he ended up dumping Margo as he had her?

"So your office manager said. Jacey will be with me all summer. So if you come by the apartment tomorrow you can meet her. I want to fly to San Francisco on Monday. If you two don't suit, I haven't a clue what I'll do. I heard you specialize in teenagers."

"I do. Is she a problem?"

"I rarely see her. Now I have her for the summer and am not sure what to do with her."

Savannah's attention was caught by his comment. Why didn't he see his daughter? He'd said he wanted to make a good family life with her. What had happened?

"What time?" she asked. Maybe she'd learn a bit more once she met Jacey.

"Say tenish?" His home address was on the questionnaire he'd filled out at the office. She knew the general area—affluent, but not outrageously so. Close to work and other amenities of downtown Manhattan. Was she seriously considering taking the assignment?

She hesitated a moment, still unable to make up her mind. She hadn't expected to be so drawn to him. They'd been lovers, always touching, kissing, delighting in just being with each other. Now it was awkward, as he'd said, to sit opposite him and pretend he was merely a client. To ignore the past, the heartache that threatened again. To refrain from demanding he tell her he'd been wrong to lose the best thing that ever happened to him.

She blinked. She was over this man!

"Tell me about the trip," she said, stalling before making up her mind. One part wanted to learn more about what he was like now. Another wanted to run as fast as she could.

"A couple of days in San Francisco, then we'll head for the Sierra Nevada mountains in California. We'll hike part of the Pacific Crest Trail for a few days to test a new tent and camping gear. Also I want to get Jacey away from New York. Her mother's made other plans this summer and she's sulking about it. The sweet little girl I knew is long gone. Now it's a phone glued to her ear, clothing that's totally inappropriate for her age and makeup that could clog a sewer pipe. All part of growing up, so Margo says, but I don't like it."

Savannah said nothing, but to her Jacey sounded like a normal teenager, maybe carrying things a bit to the extreme, but that was teenagers. And ones with divorced parents often went to the edge for attention, reassurance, love.

"Then we'll spend a few days at a resort in the mountains. It's an exclusive destination resort with hiking trails, some white-water rafting nearby and all the amenities you'd expect to find at a five-star resort." He shrugged. "I think the trip will be good for Jacey."

"Sounds like you would be with her most of the time. Why a nanny?"

"There will be times when I won't be with her. She's too young to leave on her own in San Francisco or the resort. While we're on the trail, it'll be just the three of us."

She slammed the door shut on the image that immediately sprang to mind—starlit nights, quiet conversation, kisses in the dark.

"San Francisco's a favorite city of mine," she murmured. She loved the crisp breeze from the Pacific, the dazzling white buildings against the deep blue sky. The excitement unlike New York's but special in its own way. "Has Jacey been before?"

"No. And I'm not getting an enthusiastic response when I bring it up. I'm hoping she'll come around."

He hesitated a moment, then said slowly, "There's one small thing, though." He narrowed his eyes slightly as he watched her.

Savannah's instincts clamored for caution. Something about his change in tone suggested this could be a deal breaker. Was his daughter more of a problem than a typical teenager?

"I, ah, need you to keep the past in the past. She need not know we once—" He floundered for the word, his expression one of regret.

Savannah stared at him. That was the absolutely last thing she expected. And the last thing she'd ever do—tell anyone how he'd chosen someone else over her.

"I assure you, I keep my private life my own with all my clients. I would never tell your daughter—" Never tell her of her heartbreak. Never tell her how she had so loved her father and been devastated when he'd chosen Jacey and Margo over her.

The feelings of the past threatened to swamp her. She drew a deep breath. Things changed in seven years. She was a bit disconcerted to discover she was still very aware of him as a man. But she had a life she loved, friends and a work ethic she'd spent years developing. And a definite hands-off attitude for any of her employers. She would never risk her heart a second time with a man who threw her love back in her face.

"Say something," he urged softly. "Will you take this job?"

"Why me? Surely there are others in the field you could find to accompany you two." There were other nannies in her own firm who could have gone.

"Stephanie said you had the most experience with teenagers. That you have a way with them. I need someone who will help Jacey. I think she's long overdue for some good moral values and—"

"I still have to meet her before making a decision," Savannah said. Sure, she was good enough to hire to watch his daughter for three weeks, but not good enough to marry and present as a step-mother back in the day?

"Give her a fair shot, Savannah. It wasn't her fault what happened."

She looked up and was met with steady brown eyes. What if she fell for him again?

Never! The trust they'd shared had been shattered. She would not make that mistake a second time.

For three weeks she'd have be around Declan—some of that time 24/7. She'd have to keep all thoughts of the past from mingling with the present. And she'd have to look after his daughter by another woman. She didn't know if she wanted that. It was like lemon juice hitting a cut. Sharp and painful.

Carefully putting down her cup, she prepared to leave. "I have your address from the application. We'll meet at your flat tomorrow at ten." She had to think this through. Maybe talk to Stacey or Stephanie to get an impartial view. Maybe have her head examined that she was even considering it.

"You'd need to understand about Margo, as well."

"What about her?" Savannah didn't want to even think about his wife. Ex-wife.

"We divorced before I started Murdock Sports. She left New York, but when she came back, she had Jacey. I really wanted to do the right thing by my daughter. It was a mistake from the beginning—except for Jacey. She's been the light of my world for years. However, ever since the second divorce, this company's really grown. Margo's been haranguing me for more money. She wants a share. That's the last thing I'll agree to." The hard edge of his tone reminded Savannah that as fascinating as she'd found him, he was still a hard-driven businessman.

"And she's using your daughter as a weapon," Savannah guessed. She'd dealt with other divorced parents in her job. Some could be so thoughtless around their children.

"Exactly. At least I have her for three months this summer. My hope is that we build some kind of relationship like we had a few years ago. That's the reason I wanted to start with a couple of weeks in the wilderness. Cut off from outside influences, just focusing on rebuilding our relationship, maybe she'll realize what's important in life."

There was definitely the chance to build something when it was only Jacey and her father, away from her mother, friends and cell phones.

Declan continued, "She used to love going on hikes, camping. We did a lot of it when she was younger. I'm hoping that enjoyment will surge forth again. The Sierras are the prettiest mountains in the west, I think. Clean, fresh air, beautiful country, wildlife. Perfection."

If Savannah had a lick of sense, as her grandmother used to say, she'd turn down the job so fast it'd make Declan's head swim. But she liked the outdoors. She liked to hike and camp and see nature's beauty. And she'd never seen the Pacific Crest Trail.

She was intrigued and tempted.

Yet could she set aside her resentment of his daughter? Despite his cutting her out of his life when Margo had returned, he'd helped both her and her sister and the others who now worked for Vacation Nannies by fine-tuning her business plan with her. No one else might think so, but she owed him. She had a dream job, plenty of money for her chosen lifestyle, went on assignments to some of the world's most beautiful and sought-after locations—all because Declan Murdock had taken time to teach a class.

She could handle anything for three weeks. As long as she remembered every day it was only temporary! She would be the most professional nanny in the world. And at the end of three weeks, she'd walk away without a backward look.

# CHAPTER TWO

DECLAN stared at the doorway after Savannah left. He was surprised she'd agreed to proceed. He wouldn't have blamed her if she'd refused outright.

Rubbing his hand on the back of his neck, he looked at the stack of reports in front of him. Not that he saw them. Instead, images of Savannah danced in front of his eyes. Her laughter that time they'd taken the paddle boat around the lake at St. Anne's. The way her eyes grew a deeper blue when he kissed her. The evenings they'd made dinner together, stopping between tasks to kiss, touch, promise silently that even more would come later.

The worst mistake of his life had been turning his back on Savannah, thinking he and Margo could make a marriage just for Jacey's sake.

He wasn't sure what he'd expected when he saw Savannah again, but it hadn't been that mature sophisticated businesswoman instead of the fun-loving student on the brink of life.

It looked as if she'd succeeded. He'd learned a lot about her business, but nothing about the woman. What had she been doing these past seven years beyond Vacation Nannies?

Did she have a boyfriend?

The thought twisted his gut.

He had no rights. Any he'd had years ago he'd forfeited when he'd told her goodbye.

"You need to do what you need to do and have no regrets," she'd said at that coffee shop when he'd told her he was breaking it off with her to remarry Margo.

He wished he could have lived with no regrets.

The past was past. Now he needed her in a different way—to help with his daughter.

He remembered Vacation Nannies' office manager telling him the nanny had to approve the children or they would not take the job.

He hoped Jacey would behave. He needed someone to be there for his daughter when he had to work. He'd know by tomorrow shortly after ten.

\* \* \*

The next morning Declan was up early and back at work to finish up loose ends before the trip. His housekeeper was with Jacey. She herself would be taking a vacation while he was gone. Had she been a younger woman, he would have prevailed on her to go with them to California. But, in her late fifties, she was not interested in backpacking in the mountains.

His vice president would be in charge of the business for the next few weeks. Declan knew he'd do a good job. It was hard to leave with so many different irons in the fire, but he was determined that while Jacey was with him, he'd do what he could to get his daughter comfortable around him. He wanted his sweet little girl back.

The trip was not all about bonding with Jacey. He was interested in adding an entirely new direction to the company. The fact he was combining business with their time away was prudent. He'd show his daughter some of what he did for a living, thus correlating work with earning money. Her mother was filling her head with an entitlement attitude that drove him crazy. Nothing in life came free.

Some things came with a steep price. He

thought about Savannah and couldn't help but feel a stirring of anticipation. He'd see her soon. He had told Jacey about hiring a nanny and hoped she'd behave.

He'd forgotten over the past seven years how pretty Savannah was. Or had he deliberately suppressed the memory? He'd genuinely tried to make the marriage work. It took two, however, and Margo's agenda had been different from his.

Marrying Margo a second time had been a huge mistake almost from the beginning. Granted, she was stunning. Long dark hair, mysterious eyes, a sly, catlike smile. He'd been captivated the first time around. If she'd told him she was pregnant before they'd divorced, he might have stayed in the marriage. She was high maintenance from the get-go, always wanting to party, to be seen in all the trendy places, to acquire clothes and jewelry and anything else that could be construed as a status symbol. Nothing had changed the second time they married. She'd hired a housekeeper and fobbed Jacey's care off on her.

But she hadn't told him. They'd divorced and he'd met Savannah.

She'd been a small-town girl, new to New York

and focused on the business idea she and her sister had of nannies for vacations only. He'd never felt so young and carefree as he had in the months they were together. That time still remained a special memory.

She'd been the first person he'd thought about when he decided to take Jacey backpacking in the wilderness. Savannah was no longer a shy country mouse. From her hair to her attire to her attitude, she was just what he wanted Jacey to be like when she grew up. Trendy without being over the top. Confident, assured, pleasant.

And she probably hated his guts.

He stared at the numbers in the reports he was skimming. None of them made any sense. All he could see was the cool manner in which Savannah had deliberated before giving him an answer. Her final agreement was predicated on her meeting with Jacey going well.

He checked his watch. Time to head for home. What wasn't done wouldn't get done. The world wouldn't end.

Jacey was watching television when he entered his flat a short time later. Mrs. Harris, his housekeeper, was sitting with his daughter, crocheting. Jacey looked up and then deliberately looked back at the television without any greeting.

He had to admit the all-black attire, the dark circles around her eyes and the straight, flat black hair had taken him aback when Margo had brought her by unexpectedly a week ago. Where was the sunny smile Jacey had had when she was younger? The enthusiasm she'd evidenced when she saw him? She used to run to hug him.

"Hi, Jacey," he greeted her, going across the room to give her a kiss on her cheek.

She pulled back and glared at him. "When's the babysitter coming? I called Mom. She'll want to know you plan to pawn me off on some stranger."

"Since your mother didn't consult me at all about this summer, I suspect she'll be happy enough to go along with what I have planned. I thought she was in the Hamptons."

Mrs. Harris, his housekeeper, rose and smiled at her employer. "I'll just finish up in the kitchen," she said and took off without even a glance at Jacey. She did not like confrontations and there'd already been a couple of major storms since the evening Margo had arrived unexpectedly with

Jacey, announcing she had plans for the summer and Declan could take a turn with his daughter.

Declan rarely saw Jacey. While he had visitation rights, Margo had demanded full custody. And many of the times he'd planned to see his daughter, Margo had had other plans and couldn't have Jacey spend time with him.

"She has a life, too, you know," Jacey said. "She has a hard time making ends meet. She's going to petition for more child support. And I think you could help out your only child. It's tough living in New York on a small salary."

He looked at her, hearing Margo's voice in his child's words.

"I send more than adequate child support. If she wishes to challenge it in court, maybe we should consider you coming to live with me. That way all her money could go straight to her own needs."

"I don't want to live with you. I'm stuck here this summer when I could be going to the Hamptons with Mom's friends."

He smiled without humor. "Yet your mother brought you here."

Jacey frowned. The fact was she was as angry

with her mother as much as with Declan. He was angry with Margo for putting such ideas in his daughter's head. If he could audit his ex-wife's finances, he knew he'd find more of the support money was spent on Margo than on his daughter. He knew how much he sent each month. He doubted Jacey saw much of it, however. Margo had always been high maintenance.

Jacey pouted and looked away, studying the toes of her black shoes. "I wish I was at home."

"What do you normally do at home?" he asked easily.

"Hang out with my friends, for one thing."

"Maybe when we get back from California we can see about having some come over here. Or you can visit."

"It's not like I can walk there."

"I'll provide transportation."

"Whatever."

"Until then you have San Francisco, then back-packing in the High Sierras to look forward to. Remember how we used to go camping?"

"Oh, pul-ease, not camping. I was a kid then. What did I know? When I hear California I think beaches in LA, maybe go to Hollywood, see something worth seeing."

"I understand the views from the Pacific Crest Trail in Yosemite are amazing."

The doorbell sounded. Declan took a breath. Make-or-break time.

Jacey looked at the door but didn't move.

He rose and went to open it. Savannah stood there. Today she wore a light blue silk blouse that made her eyes shimmer. Her slim white pants showed her shapely figure. He wished she'd at least smile at him instead of looking like someone going to a funeral.

Jacey came to Declan's side and looked at Savannah.

"Are you the babysitter?" she asked rudely.

"I'm a certified nanny, but you can call me a babysitter if you think that fits better," Savannah said calmly.

Jacey looked at Savannah and then at her dad. "Did you hire her for me or you?" she asked.

"That's enough," Declan snapped out. "Come in, please, Savannah. As you probably guessed, this is my daughter, Jacey." He turned to Jacey and introduced Savannah.

"If she's going, I'm not. I'm calling Mom." Jacey turned and went back to the sofa, pulling her cell phone from her pocket. She glowered at both her father and Savannah.

Savannah sighed softly. She really didn't need another assignment that didn't go well. Her last one had been enough to drive a saint crazy. And she wasn't anywhere near being a saint. While her gaze was focused on Jacey, she was very aware of the girl's father standing near enough that she caught a whiff of his aftershave, which spiraled her right back to when she'd been close enough to nuzzle his neck and be flooded with sensations of scent and touch.

Still, having come this far she felt obligated at least to give this interview a fair shake. Trying to ignore Declan, she put herself in Jacey's shoes. She found a bit of empathy. Teen years were hard. Being shunted back and forth between parents was hard. And if Jacey's mother was allowing her to dress like this, she wasn't getting a lot of parental guidance at home.

She sat on one of the chairs, looking at Jacey as the girl stared back at her.

Declan stood nearby. "Does anyone want something to drink?"

"Like what?" Jacey asked.

"Coffee, tea, hot chocolate, a soft drink?"

"I'll have coffee," Savannah said.

"I don't want anything," Jacey growled.

"I'll be right back," Declan said and disappeared into the kitchen area. Suddenly she felt sorry for Declan. He appeared to be trying so hard. Faced with the rebellious teen before her, Savannah knew he'd be in for a bumpy road.

"I don't need a babysitter," Jacey said defiantly.

Savannah took the time to study the girl while she tried to come up with an answer. Jacey could be really pretty if she'd wash her face and wash out whatever dye she'd used on her hair. And put on a colorful shirt. Black leached the color from her skin.

"I'm sure your father knows best," she ended up saying.

"I'm not going."

"Oh? Have the plans changed?"

Jacey frowned. "I don't think my mom's going to let me go to California."

Declan returned, carrying a tray with two mugs

of coffee. He glanced between the two and then placed the tray on a table. "You like it black," he said to Savannah, handing her the cup.

Jacey looked at her father with suspicion.

"Jacey says she isn't going on the trip," Savannah said, taking the cup and meeting Jacey's gaze over the rim.

"Well, Jacey's wrong. She's not only going, she's going to have a great time," he said, sitting on another chair facing the sofa.

"When Mom calls back and I tell her what you want to do, she'll come get me."

Savannah watched as she sipped her coffee. Here was a very frustrated, unhappy young person anxious to make things go her way, and they weren't going to. What could she do to distract her? Get her off that line of thinking and on to exploring the possibilities the summer offered?

Jacey faced her father defiantly. "She'll be calling soon."

"Honey, your mother said when she brought you here that she wants you to spend the summer with me. I want you to have a good time. But if you decide to make it painful, so be it. We're still going to California, all three of us."

"Did you tell her we'll be shopping in San Francisco?" Savannah asked. She looked at Jacey. "I've been to the City by the Bay before. It's a fabulous place. They have the crookedest street in the world there. Yummy seafood at the wharf. And the stores are to die for."

"Manhattan has the coolest stores," Jacey said, not at all interested.

"Other places can be cool, too, if you give them a chance," Declan said.

"I hate you!" Jacey jumped up. "Mom said you were always difficult. She was right!"

She ran from the room. A moment later a door slammed.

Savannah looked at Declan. "That went well," she said. "Not. Is she always like that?"

"Before Margo brought her over the other day, I hadn't seen her since April. The hair and makeup is new since then. I think today was a new high in rudeness. Or maybe I mean a new low. With that attitude, we're all going to be miserable."

He looked at her. "You're still going, right? I know you have the right to refuse, but see her for what she could be, not how she's acting today."

Savannah hesitated. She was a professional

and knew she was good at her job. But this assignment would be more difficult than any other she'd had. Not only was the child rebellious and going through a definite Goth stage, Savannah was having trouble not focusing on the man sitting across from her.

"I could try it. If nothing else, I'll stick through the San Francisco portion. If it is untenable you'll be on your own for the hiking part. But you'd be with her there and really not need a nanny."

He nodded. "I can handle that. It's not what I want, but if it's the best you'll offer, I'll take it. And hope you change your mind by the time we leave San Francisco."

"We don't always get what we want," Savannah said, rising. "I'll meet you at the airport on Monday. What airline and flight? I imagine the next few days will prove challenging." In more ways than dealing with his daughter.

"I think getting her away from her mother will be the best thing for her. I haven't told her yet there's no cell service in the mountains," Declan said, his expression one of bewilderment and frustration.

"Won't that be fun when she finds out,"

Savannah said. She studied Declan, seeing his frustration beneath everything. It would prove interesting to see how he handled his daughter.

Savannah hadn't known her own father; he'd died when she was very little. But she'd have loved to have had a father like Declan, good-looking, successful and obviously concerned about his daughter.

Suddenly she hoped the trip would go as planned for his sake.

She walked to the door as he rose and followed her. She could almost feel the vibrations between them. Time and distance—that's what she needed.

He looked at her and caught her gaze, lifting an eyebrow in silent question.

She looked away, too many memories.

"We leave from JFK at ten, arrive in San Francisco shortly after noon." He gave her the airline and said he could have a car pick her up.

"Not necessary, I'll be there."

She reached the door and ventured one more look at him. "Strictly business, right, Declan?"

"Absolutely. Do you want to go over the itinerary before you go?" he asked.

Savannah hesitated again, then shrugged. "I guess." Every instinct clamored for her to leave, but curiosity got the better of her.

"I have brochures and maps on the dining-room table," he said. "Jacey, come in here, please. I want to show you something."

Jacey came out of her room by the time Savannah was seated. A couple of maps were spread out on the table, a scattering of brochures nearby. Jacey sat opposite Savannah while Declan took the head seat.

"We'll fly to San Francisco Monday. We're staying right in the heart of the city. I'll take you both with me to check in with the store and get our hiking gear. Want to do anything special after that?" he asked Jacey.

When she merely shrugged, he turned to Savannah.

"There's so much to San Francisco. I think Jacey would enjoy the wharf, especially Pier 39. Then there's the crookedest street in the world, everyone should see that. We can walk down or drive, it's like a corkscrew. Chinatown's fun. And we have to ride the cable cars."

She tried to put as much enthusiasm into the

suggestions as she could. She watched Jacey as she spoke, wondering if anything would spark her interest.

"There's also some fabulous shopping around Union Square," she added.

"New York has fabulous shopping," Jacey spoke up.

Savannah nodded. "If you know where to shop."

"You don't like my clothes?" Jacey immediately took up the challenge.

"Not at all," Savannah said.

Declan frowned at her.

"What? I'm supposed to pretend I do when I don't? One thing I insist upon is absolute honesty with children," Savannah said. Time this teen learned not everyone would kowtow to her behavior.

"If you're so honest why not say you're interested in my dad and that's why you're going?"

Savannah burst out laughing. "Oh, no, you have that wrong. I'm the reluctant one on this trip"

Jacey looked at Declan, her expression puzzled. "Why?"

"Various reasons. Anyway, I'll be glad to show

you some of the attractions in San Francisco while your father's working. You can pick or I will," Savannah said.

"Whatever," Jacey mumbled, staring at the map.

"So we buy lots of stuff at your San Francisco store," Savannah said, changing the subject and looking at Declan. "I have my own boots. I don't need new ones. But a few new tops and cargo pants wouldn't hurt."

"I don't have anything like that. I don't want to go hiking," Jacey said.

"We'll have a couple of days in San Francisco, and we're ending the trip at a resort in the mountains. You'll need clothes for that, too," Declan said.

Jacey looked bored, her gaze on the map in front of her.

Savannah nodded at the maps. "Show us where we'll be hiking."

Declan rose and leaned over the map of California, showing where San Francisco was and Yosemite National Park. He drew a marker along the Pacific Crest Trail showing where it became the John Muir Trail in Yosemite.

"It's a high elevation," Savannah murmured, following as he pointed it out.

"Some of it's above ten thousand feet. And we'll have higher peaks surrounding us."

"Where are we staying?" Jacey asked, leaning forward to look.

"Camping out on the trail. We'll backpack our stuff—clothes, tent, sleeping bags, food, everything. This is true wilderness. But the resort is here," Declan said, pointing to a spot on the map not too far from Yosemite National Park.

Jacey pulled out her cell phone to check it. "Mom should be calling me," she said.

"Maybe your mother has already started her summer," Declan said.

"What does that mean?" she asked suspiciously.

"She obviously had plans this summer that didn't include you. Why else would you be here for three months?"

"She likes to have me there."

"I know she does. But she's an adult and would like some time to herself," Declan said.

"She can't do much. She has to work all the time. We don't have money for extras," Jacey said.

"I have to work," he said easily.

"Most people on the planet have to work," Savannah added. Wow, Margo had done a number on this child. Money wasn't that important in the greater scheme of things. Family, friends, experiences, all went together to make a rich, fulfilling life. Money helped, but there was more to life than money.

"You're rich, you could do more for us," Jacey said to her father, ignoring Savannah.

"What more do you want, Jacey?" he asked, looking directly at her.

"We're always pinching pennies," she grumbled.

"I send your mother a lot of money each month. It's supposed to all go for you. What're you lacking that my generous child support doesn't provide?" he asked.

"I didn't go skiing with my friends in February. Mom said we didn't have enough money and you wouldn't give her any more."

"You're old enough to understand a few things," Declan said. "First we'll discuss the money I send." He told her how much money he sent each month. Judging from the way Jacey's eyes widened, she'd had no idea. "Granted, some of it goes to supplement the rent and food and basic expenses like that. But if your mother managed the money well, there'd be plenty for extras like a ski trip in February. And, by the way, this is the first time I've heard about that."

"It's expensive to live in New York," Jacey said.

"Your mother's not managing the money I'm sending. Next time something like that comes up, call me directly. I'll consider paying for the trip."

"Mom needs money this summer," she said.

"Now isn't that interesting? I continue to pay the same amount every month, no reduction for the time you stay with me."

Declan glanced at Savannah who was watching the interchange closely. He disliked airing dirty laundry in front of strangers, not that she was a stranger precisely, but he didn't know her now. She'd changed over the years. He hadn't a clue what she was thinking. Probably that all his problems served him right. He'd made a major mistake and could never forget that.

"So we leave in two days," she said, trying to change the subject.

He nodded, suddenly wondering if his idea had been such a good one after all. Jacey was behaving worse than he'd expected. He hoped their time together would prove beneficial.

What really startled him was the anticipation he felt at the thought of spending the next three weeks with Savannah Williams. She'd done nothing even to hint she wanted to resume a friendship, much less anything more. And he couldn't blame her. Looking back, he'd shattered something precious.

No one could go back to the past. Knowing what he now knew, he'd have held on to Savannah for all he was worth.

What would it be like to take this trip with her? What if they could have taken it alone? Spend days hiking spectacular country and then nights with nothing but the starry sky overhead and endless miles of empty land surrounding them? He knew the reality of their trip would be different, but, for a moment, he almost pretended.

# CHAPTER THREE

TIME flew by and before she knew it Savannah was boarding a plane for the flight to San Francisco Monday morning. All weekend she'd dithered, talking things through with Stephanie because she couldn't reach her sister. In the end, she decided to go. It might be a mistake, but she'd made plenty of those in her life. What was one more?

Declan had booked three seats in first class, a luxury she'd grown used to in her line of work. Most of the families who could afford Vacation Nannies had plenty of money and wanted their children to enjoy first-class travel as much as they did—as long as the nanny was there to watch them.

Sitting by the window, Savannah settled in with pleasure. Her lifestyle was so different today from what she'd experienced growing up in that small house on the outskirts of Palmerville, West Virginia.

"Want to sit by the window?" Declan asked Jacey when they boarded the plane.

"Whatever," she said, going in first. Their two seats were together. Savannah's was across the aisle.

Settling in, they watched as the rest of the passengers for the flight boarded. Once they were airborne, Declan got out of his seat and leaned over to talk to Savannah.

"There was a mix-up in the room reservation at the hotel in San Francisco. We have a suite, but only two bedrooms. Would you find it horrible to share with Jacey? I was confirmed for a larger suite, but found out this morning we got bumped to the smaller one. Some special envoy or something."

She looked into his dark eyes. He looked tired. How stressful was it having his teenage daughter fighting him at every step? Jacey stared out the window, looking mad and unhappy.

"That's what you've hired me for, to be with Jacey. It'll be fine."

"Thanks. If she says anything—I mean, I expect she'll be a bit of a brat."

"Remember you asked for a teen expert. I've handled recalcitrant teenagers before. Relax, Declan. She's being a teenager. They really do better with boundaries and adults running the show. Start as you mean to go on."

He nodded and sat back in his seat.

Savannah smiled at her seat companion and turned to gaze out the window. She had her own problems. Like not getting to sleep last night for thinking about the trip with Declan Murdock. She'd been so in love with him years ago. She thought she'd put all romantic notions behind her when he left. But he was even more interesting now that she'd seen more of the world, spent time among dynamic men who moved in the highest circles. He had a special appeal, and it wasn't all based on the past.

Declan could hire a raft of people to watch his daughter. But he'd chosen her. Not for old times' sake, but because she'd come so highly recommended. And he did need help with his daughter if he so rarely saw her. Savannah was here to do a job, not to dream about her temporary employer.

Savannah brought out a novel she'd picked up in Boston, not having had a moment to read it after she'd landed in New York—was it only a couple of days earlier? Reading would while away the flight.

As they prepared to land several hours later, Savannah looked over to see Jacey peering out the window as the plane banked over San Francisco. The city gleamed in the sunshine. The buildings of downtown were predominantly white. The water of the San Francisco Bay were deep blue. It was a gorgeous day. Savannah hoped that the teenager would let herself experience some emotion at visiting one of the world's most exciting and beautiful cities.

When they reached the hotel near Union Square, Savannah was pleased with the ease at which Jacey accepted the room assignments. They went into the room they'd share. Two double beds left plenty of room for a dresser and television. The sitting room of the suite also had a large-screen television and two sofas, several easy chairs and a wet bar.

They had a small view of Union Square and when they opened the old-fashioned window, they could hear the famous cable cars clanging as they reached the turntable near Market Street.

Jacey plopped on her bed and leaned back, staring at the ceiling.

"It's only midafternoon. Want to go out?" Savannah asked. The advantage of traveling west was arriving in time to do things.

"Is Dad going?"

"He said he wants to go to the store right away. We could go with him. Or wait until tomorrow to go shopping for our hiking stuff. I know a couple of places where we could find some trendy clothes. Maiden Lane has some fabulous shops."

Jacey sat up. "Whatever."

Savannah resisted rolling her eyes. She wished that word had never been invented. However, she was sure Jacey and teens everywhere would find another equally annoying if that were the case.

Shopping proved more fun than Savannah had expected. In the first shop, Savannah pulled out a lollipop-pink sundress. "My sister's favorite color is pink," Savannah said. "I wouldn't be caught dead in this."

"If you were dead, you wouldn't know what you were wearing," Jacey said.

Savannah laughed. So maybe the kid could be fun to be around. "Good point. What's your favorite color—and don't say black."

"What if that's my favorite color?"

"It's no one's favorite color. Lots of people wear it, but not because it's a favorite color. Purple's my favorite, but I don't wear a lot of it."

"Why not?"

"I don't want to look like a plum?" Savannah suggested.

Jacey actually giggled. "I'd like to see you in purple."

"Okay, find something. I'm not buying, but I'll try it on."

Jacey searched through dresses, finally finding a deep purple one.

"Okay, wait here." Hoping she could trust the teen not to dart away as soon as her back was turned, Savannah went to the changing room. Stepping out a couple of minutes later she was relieved to see Jacey still looking at dresses.

Turning to see Savannah, Jacey began to laugh. "You do look like a tall, thin plum."

"You try it on and see what you look like, Miss Smarty-Pants. You'd look like a plum, too,"

Savannah retorted, delighted to finally hear a laugh from the girl.

"Purple's not my favorite color."

"What is, then?"

"Blue."

"Powder, navy, aqua?"

"Powder."

Savannah pulled out a light blue dress. "So try it on. Maybe you'll look like a robin's egg."

Jacey rolled her eyes but followed Savannah back to the dressing rooms. While Savannah changed back into the outfit she'd worn on the plane she could hear clothing shuffle in the changing stall next to hers. She was surprised to see how pretty Jacey looked when she stepped out in the blue dress. The makeup was still garish, the hair too dark, but she looked more like a pretty young girl.

"Nice," Savannah said casually. "Want to try on another dress? We don't have to buy anything. It's fun to play dress-up. You should've seen me and my sister when we first moved to New York. We'd spend all Saturday afternoon shopping at high-end stores, just trying on clothes."

They'd done it to find out what looked good

and what didn't, making notes on what styles best suited each of them. It made a big difference in the way two country girls were able finally to fit in.

Over the next hour Jacey tried on several different outfits, but she never returned the blue one to the rack.

As it grew closer to the time to meet Declan for dinner, Savannah wondered if she dare buy the blue dress for Jacey.

"Ready to go?" she asked.

"I guess. This has been fun. I think I could be a model."

"Sure, once you learn the tricks of the trade."

"Like?"

"How to walk, pivot, fix your hair and makeup." She was taking a chance very early in their tenuous relationship, but Savannah only had three weeks with Jacey, if that. Anything she could do for Declan would be worth the risk. "Maybe we could get a makeover at one of the department stores on Union Square. I bet their makeup selection is huge."

"Ummm." Jacey didn't exactly jump at the

chance, but Savannah was relieved not to have her turn it down completely.

"I like the blue dress," Jacey said casually.

"I do, too. Shall we buy it?" She held her breath.

"Whatever."

Savannah laughed. "Deal."

They reached their hotel room before Declan returned.

"Time for a shower and shampoo before dinner," Savannah said when Jacey dropped the bag from the store on her bed. "Want to go first?"

"I guess. You could use Dad's bathroom since he isn't here," she suggested. "Then I can take as long a shower as I want."

She was once again trying to reach her mother by phone. Savannah didn't know if Margo had ever called her daughter over the weekend. If not, Jacey must be getting annoyed at being ignored.

"Okay, that'll work," she said. Judging how much longer until the dinner time Declan had suggested, she figured she'd have time to be in and out before he returned.

Savannah walked through Declan's bedroom to his bath a few moments later. She kept her gaze averted from the bed, ignoring the few things of his on the dresser. But stepping into the bathroom brought back even more memories. His scent permeated the air. She saw his razor on the bath counter, his aftershave in a bottle beside it. For a moment she was immobile, remembering.

Shaking off the past, she stepped into the shower and soon felt the soothing beat of the hot water. *Focus on your job,* she admonished herself. Jacey had been cordial most of the afternoon—actually, almost friendly toward the end. Trying on clothes was fun no matter what kind of attitude she was trying to maintain.

Still, it felt good to have a few moments to herself. She wondered what Declan had been doing while they shopped. Not that she cared. Maybe she should suggest he take Jacey to dinner and let her stay behind to order room service. It would give the two of them time alone. And she would be spared dining with him again.

Not him precisely. Nothing like before. Despite all the pep talks she'd given herself, it was hard not to feel something around him. An innate curiosity, a feeling of déjà vu, an attraction that sprang forth as strong as ever before. And a memory of his hard words, the end of her love.

After drying off a few moments later, Savannah slipped on one of the thick terry robes the hotel provided. She towel-dried her hair, needing to get the mousse on it. Now it was flat and boring. She didn't know how her sister stood having such long hair. Short hair was so easy to care for. And she liked the sassy look it gave her.

Opening the door she stopped suddenly when she saw Declan lying on the bed. His legs were crossed at the ankles, one arm under his head, as he stared at her coming from his bathroom. Heat flooded, her heart raced. So he'd looked many times before when they'd spent a weekend some-where. Swallowing hard, she tried to breathe.

"Oh."

"Oh, indeed," he said, rising. He crossed slowly over to her as his gaze traveled down the length of the terry robe. Her heart flipped over, pounded harder than ever.

"Jacey and I wanted showers before dinner. You weren't here. I hope I didn't hold you up," she said. She also hoped he wasn't getting any ideas about her appropriating his bathroom. Obviously she'd misjudged how long he'd be at the store.

He stopped inches away. She wore only the robe, closed with a sash that with one flick of a wrist could be undone. Trying not to think of how little she had on beneath the robe—like, nothing but bare skin—she edged sideways toward the door. He stepped closer and for a split second she thought he was going to reach for her. The surge of longing to feel his arms around her one more time caught her by surprise. Her gaze flicked to his mouth, her own almost tingling in yearning to feel those lips against her again, drawing a response from her that she'd once so freely given.

Then the echo of the words he'd said that had ended everything sounded in her mind.

She was fantasizing about him ripping off the robe and taking her into his arms, kissing her for real, a full-blown lip lock that would blow her mind, when he'd so cavalierly thrown her over for Margo. Now Margo was gone. Did he think he could step back in where they'd left off?

She took another step, watching him warily. What could she say to make sure he knew she was so over him it wasn't funny? That she'd taken this job only for Jacey's sake.

Declan stepped closer. She could feel the warmth from his body. Her eyes locked with his as her imagination ran wild.

"Declan," she started, but that husky voice didn't sound like the crisp professional tone she was striving for. She cleared her throat, took two more steps to the door and opened it.

"How did it go with Jacey today?" he asked.

She turned and looked at him over her shoulder.

"Actually, better than I expected. She actually thawed a bit by the time we reached the second store. I had her trying on any dress she wanted as long as it wasn't black. She even let me buy her a blue one. If she wears it tonight, be complimentary, but don't make a big deal over it."

"Any luck with the makeup?"

"Young girls need to experiment. I'd say you have a typical teen. Once in the wilderness, no makeup for a few days and a compliment or two thrown her way, and I bet she doesn't go back to it. I suggested we could go to one of the major department stores and have a makeover. But her response was tepid at best. Maybe when she gets back to New York you can take her to one of the stores there."

"The resort has a day spa connected. She could go there." He checked his watch. "I have reservations for seven at a place in North Beach."

"I thought maybe you and Jacey should go alone. More time for you to get better acquainted with what she's been up to lately," Savannah said. Even more than before she wanted some distance from Declan. Using his bathroom had been another mistake. She needed to keep tabs and change her behavior or she risked serious heartbreak again.

He stared at her for a long moment, then shook his head. "I need you to buffer."

Savannah shivered and shrugged. "Okay. We'll be ready." Scooting away, she tried to ignore the aching longing that seemed to invade every cell. Why did she have such a hard time remembering he had been the one to end their relationship years ago? How could she let herself be snared by his attractiveness again? Once burned, she needed to guard her defenses.

But for a moment, she could almost feel his mouth on hers.

Jacey was standing in front of the full-length mirror studying herself when Savannah almost burst into their bedroom. She wore a slinky black dress with spaghetti straps and an uneven swirling hemline. Her midnight-black hair hung straight down her back. She had not yet put on the makeup and her sweet face looked pale and drawn against all the black. Savannah couldn't help but wonder why Jacey couldn't see that black was not her color.

She spun around when Savannah entered. "I thought you and my dad would be longer," she said. "I heard him come in a few minutes ago."

"I finished my shower, now it's his turn," Savannah responded, going to the closet to pull out a silvery dress. Black didn't look good with her fair coloring so she rarely wore it. This color was a smoky silvery gray, and looked great with her eyes. To her, the best feature was how well the dress traveled. She glanced at Jacey and considered telling her to put a shirt on, but Jacey wasn't her child and she wasn't going to get into a free-for-all over clothes. If her mother didn't have better taste in clothes for a fourteen-year-old, Savannah hoped her father would.

BARBARA McMAHON                    71

"I've got to get my hair done," she said, heading for their en suite bath. "You finished in here for a bit?"

"I need to do my makeup, but I can wait until you're done," Jacey called, turning back to the mirror.

Savannah truly hoped the child hated what she saw. Once she had on her macabre makeup, she'd look like the wicked witch from the *Wizard of Oz*.

Savannah had to get her own hair and makeup under control. Shouldn't she get hazardous-duty pay for even contemplating trying to change a teenager? She saw Jacey's clutter on the bathroom counter. The black eyeliner and mascara and the bright rosy blush. Tempting though it was to hide everything, Savannah resisted. She had to get the girl to want to change, not force it on her.

Once dressed, Savannah went into the lounge to give Jacey the bedroom and bath to herself. She walked to the window to enjoy the slight view of Union Square. One of the renowned cable cars was passing. She hoped they got to ride one from one end to another. How could Jacey be blasé about that?

Declan stepped into the lounge. Savannah

turned and her eyes widened slightly. He looked amazing. The dark suit contrasted with the snowy shirt and maroon tie. He looked like the very successful businessman he was. His gaze went to her immediately. For a second Savannah could imagine that the two of them were going to dinner and she'd dressed her best to please him.

"You look lovely," he said.

No employer had to say that! "Thank you, I could say the same. Be warned, Morticia will be joining us for dinner."

He grimaced. "Didn't wear the blue dress?"

"Nope."

He ran his hand across the back of his neck. "I don't understand what Margo's thinking, letting her dress that way."

"She thinks she looks sophisticated. Does your ex-wife wear a lot of black?

"I don't know what she does these days. She didn't, back when we were married."

"Well, I think this is a stage," Savannah said.

The bedroom door opened and Jacey walked out. Her eyes were heavily lined in black, her hair had been teased a bit and looked more like a black football helmet than anything else. The high heels she wore made Savannah wonder how she didn't teeter over and fall on her face. She turned back to look at Declan and almost laughed aloud at his dismayed expression.

"So, now we're all ready," she said brightly, hoping to catch his eye.

He looked at her. "Not—"

"—a minute too soon, I know."

Fortunately Declan caught on fast. "Right. Then, if we're all ready, I have reservations at a good restaurant in Little Italy. Everyone likes Italian, right?"

"Sounds wonderful," Savannah said. She glanced at Jacey and felt a moment of sympathy for the girl. Did she even know what she wanted?

Declan bowed to Savannah's hints, but his initial reaction had been to send Jacey back to her room to wash her face. How could Margo let their precious little girl end up like this? The dress was totally inappropriate for someone so young. And a bit over the top for the restaurant they were going to. Some wild night club would be more suitable for the dress—not his daughter.

Savannah looked lovely. Why couldn't Jacey want to look like her?

The cab took them swiftly through the San Francisco traffic and they arrived at the restaurant just before seven. Once seated, Jacey looked around with a frown. Declan watched her. One of the things he and Margo had enjoyed was dining out. Of course, back then, they hadn't had a lot of money. With what he sent each month, she could still enjoy a dinner out from time to time. Did she never take their daughter? Jacey seemed to be bemused by all she saw.

"Do they have pizza?" Jacey asked.

"I'm sure they do," Savannah said. "Did you know the flatbread food we call pizza only had tomato sauce after the Spanish conquistadors brought tomatoes to Europe?"

"What is this? A history lesson?" Jacey asked.

Savannah laughed. "Sorry, my sister and I are always trying to find out obscure facts to dazzle the other one with. Sometimes that spills over."

"I didn't know it," Declan said. "In fact, I didn't know tomatoes were indigenous to America."

"South America, actually, though the Spaniards

spread them all around. Since we've grown up eating tomatoes, I, for one, never questioned where they originated before I went to college." She folded her menu and smiled at him. "But in a fine restaurant like this one, I want more than pizza. I'll have the linguine Alfredo."

"I'm having the veal," he said.

He glanced at Jacey "Pizza's fine if that's what you want."

She closed her menu and looked around. The uncertainty and vulnerable look tugged at his heart.

"Tomorrow we'll go to the store and pick out some clothes for our hike," he said once the order had been taken.

"I still don't see why I have to go," Jacey said. "Why don't you leave me and Savannah here and go on without us? Camping's not fun."

"You used to enjoy camping," he said.

"Well, I enjoyed a lot of different things when I was a kid. I'd like to stay in San Francisco, if we're not going back to New York right away."

"So tell me about camping. Where did you two used to go?" Savannah said.

"The Adirondacks, Poconos, nothing like western mountains. Remember, Jacey, we'd take off after school on Fridays, get a good spot. Then we'd hike, swim if it was warm enough to. Or we'd follow a trail looking for wildlife. Evenings we'd have a campfire and roast marshmallows." Declan spoke about several of their trips.

Savannah watched as the happy memories spilled from him. When she'd glance at Jacey she didn't see fond memories. Why couldn't she unbend long enough to agree with her father about the fun they used to have?

"One more day here in the city and then we leave," Declan said. "I sure am looking forward to the Pacific Crest Trail."

"Me, too." Savannah said. "I brought my hiking boots and some old clothes, but I don't mind buying a few new things. I'd love to see your store here. I've been in the one in Manhattan. Do you have different things for sale in different stores?"

"Depends on where the store is located. For instance, we have more surfboards for sale on the west coast than in our east-coast stores. We can ship in anything from our catalogue, but we don't normally stock surfboards in Manhattan."

Jacey played with her silverware, looking totally bored.

"Remember, Jacey, when you used to come to the store and play with all the balls we had?" Declan said in an effort to include her in the conversation.

She shrugged. Looking at Savannah, she asked, "What do you get out of being a nanny?"

"Actually, quite a lot of enjoyment and a chance to travel. I'm co-owner of the business with my sister, Stacey. We make enough to live the lifestyle we like, and we don't need to depend on anyone else."

"Unlike your mother," Declan murmured.

Jacey turned and glared at him. "She works. They don't pay well in New York."

"I make a comfortable living, Savannah makes a comfortable living. Your mother could if she wanted," Declan said.

"She has an image to uphold. That doesn't come cheap," Jacey defended.

"An image?" Savannah asked. Was this a clue to getting closer to Jacey?

"She works in a very exclusive boutique and has to look the part. Even with ten percent off the clothes she buys, they're incredibly expensive." Jacey looked at her father. "You can't say our apartment's glamorous. It's barely in an acceptable area."

"I'm not discussing your mother's life with you. If you have a problem with her, you talk to her."

"I don't have a problem with her—it's you. You have millions. You could be a little more generous to your only daughter!" Jacey almost shouted the last.

Heads turned, eyes searched for the source, then were averted when Declan glared around the restaurant.

Savannah almost reached out and touched the back of the fist he had clenched on the table. He took a breath and looked at her. He was furious.

Savannah wanted to help. She turned to Jacey.

"So your mother's a buyer in an exclusive boutique dress shop?"

"She's a sales clerk. But if they'd give her the chance, she'd be a buyer. Until then she has to sell clothes to rich people like she'd be if Dad would send more money. He's loaded."

Savannah nodded. She could hear the echo of Declan's ex-wife in those words.

Just then Jacey's phone rang. She snatched it out of her purse, checked the number calling, then opened it eagerly. "Mom, where have you been? I've been calling and calling."

"Jacey, not at the table," Declan said.

She glared at him. "Hold on, Dad doesn't want me talking to you."

"That's not what I said," he said with restraint. "Take it in the lobby so you aren't disturbing the other customers."

"Like I care about them," she mumbled as she rose and quickly headed for the lobby.

"So her mother doesn't call as often as Jacey wants?" Savannah asked as the teen quickly walked away from their table.

"Margo hasn't talked to Jacey since she dropped her at the apartment. And since your interview, Jacey's called her a dozen times with no response until now. Despite what Jacey says, Margo wanted this summer for her own ends."

"If she works at a high-end shop, shouldn't she know better how to dress her daughter?"

"I'm sure she does, but it's easier to let Jacey do her own thing. Margo wasn't much on discipline when we lived together. I expect nothing's changed. I wish she'd stop filling Jacey's head with the idea I owe them more money. I send child support, I'm not planning to support Margo in the lifestyle she'd like."

Savannah nodded. She did not want to get involved in the family dynamics. She wondered how things would have gone if he hadn't tried a second marriage with Margo. Would they have found an easier way to relate, or would Jacey still be going through this stage? This trip was not going to be as easy as Declan thought.

The waiter had begun to serve their plates when Jacey came back.

"Mom was at the Hamptons this weekend. She left her phone at home," she said, slipping into her chair. She looked at Savannah. "She said she didn't know about you."

"Why would she? We live different lives," Declan said easily.

Savannah was glad to see he'd regained his composure. He'd been angry with his daughter but had let it go. She suspected there would be a lot of that in the days to come.

"I think you and Mom should get back together," she said, challenging her father with her look.

Savannah glanced at Declan.

"It's never going to happen, Jace. Your mother and I tried that when she came back to New York with you. You know that. Eat up. I'll satisfy your clothing requirements at the store tomorrow. You can buy anything you want."

Savannah wondered how much black hiking gear would be found.

"I still don't want to go. Don't I count for anything?" she said sulkily.

"You count for a lot. But the plans are made. I hope you'll remember how much you liked camping when you were little. We'd see deer and beavers and other wildlife."

She shrugged. "Big whoop. I can see animals in the zoo."

"I hope we see them. I can go to the zoo, too, but would love to see some in the wild," Savannah said. "What's your favorite animal?"

The rest of the meal passed pleasantly with Savannah doing her best to draw Jacey out, and Declan paying close attention to all Jacey said. Gradually the conversation grew broader. He told her about his favorite tourist attraction in San Francisco, what he hoped to see while hiking. And how she and Savannah could help evaluate the products he was testing.

"I want the tent to be easy enough for novice hikers as well as suitable for seasoned backpackers," he said.

Jacey listened but didn't say anything. Savannah thought she saw a spark of interest when Declan talked about evaluations, but she wasn't sure. *Something* had to interest this child.

When they were finished, Declan called a cab to return to the hotel. As the three of them rode silently up in the elevator, Savannah wondered if she was helping in any way. The two didn't seem a bit closer than they had been when she'd first met Jacey. And the tension in the elevator car was thick enough to cut with a knife. She still had another day or two to decide whether to stay the course or to return to New York when they headed for the hiking trail. If she had to decide right now, Savannah would opt for home.

# CHAPTER FOUR

THE next morning Savannah woke early. Jacey was still sleeping, so she kept as quiet as possible while she dressed. It was awful to feel this way, but she didn't want to confront the teen any earlier than she had to. This was not going to be the dream assignment she always hoped for.

Slipping into the lounge once dressed, she was surprised to find Declan fully dressed, an empty plate beside him, sipping coffee as he studied his laptop. For a moment she wanted to turn and slide back into the bedroom.

He looked up before she could do so. "Good morning. Sleep well?"

"Yes. I'm still on New York time I guess."

"Me, too. I've already eaten. Call room service and order breakfast. I'm catching up on some work. Tomorrow we head for the mountains and I'll be out of touch for a while." He studied her for a moment, then looked back at the computer.

"Actually, I thought I'd take a quick walk around Union Square before the day fully starts. By the time I get back, Jacey might be up and we can eat together." She headed for the door, anxious to escape.

"Sure." He leaned back in the chair and looked at her. "Sorry she was such a brat last night."

Savannah shrugged. "I've handled worse. Teen years are hard."

"Yet that's your age specialty, so I was told."

"It is. They are hard sometimes, but other times, I see amazing transformations and that makes it all worthwhile. Plus I remember being a teenager and all the angst that goes with it. Especially if one is out of step with others in her peer group. I took several courses on adolescent behavior. Wow, that was an eye-opener. I could have applied what I learned to my own life. So I figure I'm a good advocate for them."

"As I remember, you came from a small town in West Virginia."

She nodded, remembering all the things they'd shared. "Palmerville. How did you remember that?"

He looked at her directly. "I never forgot one

thing about you, Savannah. I remember your goal was to make enough money to live well. It looks as if you succeeded at that."

She nodded. "We've done what we set out to do. My sister and I have all we wanted. Our company's growing, both in reputation and in the number of nannies who now work for us. The apartment we have isn't in the best of neighborhoods, but since we're rarely home more than a couple of days at a time, it suits us."

"Do you really travel that much?"

"Spring, summer and holidays, yes, I'm gone most of the time. But I love it. I've been on every continent except Antarctica. I've been to carnival in Rio, seen the Pope's blessing in Rome, visited Uluru in Australia. What's not to like?"

He nodded. "Margo should try something like that. It might assuage her desire for expensive life experiences."

She didn't want to discuss his wife. Or even to remember he'd chosen Margo over her when she'd been so very much in love with him. And had thought for a few glorious months that he'd loved her.

"I need to go," she said, opening the door.

"The store opens at ten. I have nothing planned before then, so I'll be here when Jacey wakes," he said.

Out into the hall, she felt as if she'd already gone for a run. Being around Declan was not getting easier, she thought, gulping air. *He remembered everything about me.*

Truth to tell, she remembered every minute they'd spent together. The walks around Central Park, watching skaters at Rockefeller Center at Christmas, even helping out when he had that bad case of strep throat. Tears filled her eyes and angrily she dashed them away. Tough times, but gone. Head held high, she walked to the elevator.

Savannah loved San Francisco. She'd visited each September for the past three years with the Thompson family and their children, Sean and Irene. The children loved riding on the cable cars, exploring Fisherman's Wharf and the Exploratorium. They were still at a fun age. This year they'd be ten and eleven. Approaching the dreaded teen years, but still young enough not to have attitudes that sometimes drove her crazy.

She stepped out of the hotel and headed for Union Square. There was a crispness in the air due to the marine fog. San Francisco wasn't exactly a hot spot in summer as the marine fog kept the temperatures cooler than New York. But it felt good today. The park was tiny compared to Central Park, but it offered a spot of green surrounded by high-rises. The breeze was cool. Setting off briskly, Savannah almost did a quick dance step. It was a beautiful day and she was in her favorite city.

When she returned to their suite thirty minutes later, Jacey was sitting on a chair, one leg slung over the arm, reading a book. Declan was still at his computer. The teen looked up when Savannah entered.

"I'm starved. Dad said I had to wait for you to eat."

"I'm sorry. I should have told you I have my cell. You could have called to let me know you were up. Maybe tomorrow if you're still sleeping I'll wake you up. You could have come with me, it's gorgeous out."

"Dad says we'll walk to the store from here. I'm hungry."

"Be good exercise and preparation for the trail," Declan said with a smile for his daughter.

"I still don't want to go," Jacey said.

Savannah didn't feel she was any closer to getting to know Jacey than when they'd started. The hours were ticking down to decision time. Did she plan to extend her stay, or leave to return home when Declan and his daughter left for the backpacking trek?

When they entered the Murdock Sports store shortly after ten, Savannah compared it to the one she'd visited in Manhattan. This one was larger. The staff was young and friendly. Each sales clerk she saw looked as if he or she had just come in from running or biking or surfing. A healthy glow and trim body epitomized each one.

Declan introduced Jacey and Savannah to the manager, who in turn called one of her most knowledgeable staff members to assist. When Declan went back to the office with the manager, Savannah and Jacey went with their guide to search for their supplies and clothes.

As Savannah had suspected, there was very little in black.

Savannah quickly picked out several shirts and cargo pants to try on. She waited as Jacey listlessly pushed the hangers along or looked through the shirts folded on shelves.

"Don't see anything you like?" she asked after a few minutes.

"I don't know why I have to do this. I'd rather be in New York with Mom."

"What would you be doing there?" Savannah asked. "I thought your mother worked."

"She does. I'd watch TV until she gets home."

"And then?"

She shrugged. "Hang out, I guess."

"Instead, now you have the opportunity to see an amazing national park, with views I hear are spectacular. A entire week to be out in the fresh air and sunshine and do something rather than sit around."

Jacey looked at her, eyes narrowed. "Are you a PE teacher?"

Savannah laughed. "Hardly. But you're young. Don't you like to keep your body moving? I'm excited about the trip—to see the scenery I've only heard about."

Jacey looked at her a moment, then looked back at the shirts. She picked up a navy one, the closest thing to black on the shelf. "I guess I'll take this one."

"We're not going to be able to wash clothes where we're going so if they get sweaty or dirty, you don't want to wear one more than a day. You need a week's worth," Savannah said.

Grumbling, Jacey picked out another couple of colors and bought two shirts in each color. The sales clerk would earn her salary for today, Savannah thought, as she almost pushed Jacey into getting all the clothes she needed. A hint of enthusiasm or gratitude wouldn't go amiss.

Declan joined them when almost everything had been tried on and decided upon. He went to Jacey and rested his arm across her shoulders. She seemed surprised by the gesture but didn't shake him off.

"How are you doing?"

"I picked out what I want. Savannah said there won't be any washing machines, so I got enough for every day."

She held out the stack of shirts in her hands in navy, pink, yellow and minty green. Savannah didn't say a word, but the look she shared with

Declan behind Jacey's back signaled progress with colors.

When they went to the register, Savannah took her clothes to a different clerk from the one Declan stopped at.

"I'll buy those," he called over.

"I'll buy my own clothes, thank you," she said, pulling out her credit card. This was strictly business and she wasn't going to confuse the issue no matter what Declan thought. Even back when they'd been a couple she had paid her way many times. She never wanted to be totally dependent on anyone.

In the cab back to the hotel, Jacey asked Savannah why she hadn't let her dad buy her clothes.

"First, it's inappropriate. Second, I told you, I'm capable of supporting myself, I don't need anyone else helping me."

"He's paying you to babysit me, why not let him pay for the clothes you need for that job?"

Savannah wanted to ask if her mother took stuff, but that would be too personal. "He's paying me to do my job," she said. "I pay my own way when it comes to everything else."

"So you're really not looking for my dad to be your meal ticket," Jacey asked, confused.

Savannah laughed. If she only knew. "Nope."

Obviously the idea was new to Declan's daughter.

Savannah wondered what life lessons she was learning from her mother. Maybe Declan should explore obtaining custody of her during her impressionable teen years.

When they'd sent their new clothes into the hotel laundry, with a guarantee they'd be ready the next morning, Declan asked Jacey what she wanted to do for the rest of the day.

"Whatever."

"So maybe we could look at the maps again to see where we're going, talk about the trek?" he suggested.

"Boring," Jacey said. "Can we go ride the cable cars?"

"I thought you didn't want to go sightseeing?" Declan said.

"Better than staying here and looking at maps," she said.

"How about you?" he asked Savannah.

"I've a few things to do. You two don't need me for that. Go, have fun."

He raised an eyebrow in surprise. What could she have to do? Not go with him, that was obvious. He wondered what it would be like if she weren't here almost under duress. If she still enjoyed time spent with him.

Of course, any fantasies he entertained surrounding Savannah would not include a fourteen-year-old daughter tagging along.

Not that he needed to be having any fantasies right now. He was here for Jacey. He still couldn't believe Savannah had gone along with his job offer. Sometimes—like once or twice a minute—he wished he could turn back the clock. Make a different choice seven years ago.

"Then let's go ride a San Francisco landmark," he said. With enough distractions, he could forget about his growing awareness of his daughter's nanny.

"Why do I have to go if the babysitter doesn't?" Jacey asked.

"Savannah is entitled to some time off. It'll just be you and me."

The rest of the day proved to be the most fun

Declan had had with his daughter in a long time. By the time their cable car reached Fisherman's Wharf, Jacey had seemed to forget her surly teenage persona and thrown herself into the ride. The wind blew from the Bay as they walked to Pier 39 and all the shops and restaurants there. For a few moments, he caught a glimpse of his little girl. She laughed once at two little girls holding on to their carousel horses and waving at their parents from the carousel.

They stepped into the chocolate store and browsed the endless array of chocolates. A short time later, strolling along eating delicious chocolate truffles, Declan almost recaptured those first years with the child he hadn't known about. She'd been adorable at seven when they'd first met. And even until last year, he'd thought they had a special bond.

Jacey was especially enthralled with the sea lions that had appropriated several docks. When hoarse barking drew them along the pier, she laughed aloud at the fat animals. Declan thought he could have stayed there forever, watching his daughter make faces at the sea creatures, hearing her laugh, enjoying the perfect weather.

They ate fish and chips for an early dinner, strolled back along the wharf, watching those who were flying kites in the brisk afternoon breeze. The elaborate structures swerved, dipped and soared on the constant sea breeze.

Riding the cable car back to downtown, Jacey stood on the running board, holding on to one of the poles. She'd lean back and let the wind blow through her hair and Declan feared she'd fall off. But her enjoyment kept his mouth shut with cautions.

Still, he was glad when they reached their hotel suite safe and sound.

"I'm going to call Mom," Jacey said heading to the bedroom.

Declan went to sit on the sofa, leaning aback against the cushions. Savannah wasn't here. What had she to do in San Francisco? Did she have friends here? A special someone?

He frowned, not liking that thought. Since Margo, he'd been very wary of getting involved with anyone. Business gave him plenty to do and, until the past few months, he had tried to see Jacey as much as possible.

Still, being around Savannah, seeing her reserve after remembering the carefree, loving woman he'd known before, hurt. He knew he was the reason for that wariness and he hated himself for causing such a change.

And for thinking he was doing right at the time to try to make a family for his daughter. The two years he and Margo had been together that time had probably been almost worse for Jacey than if he'd been a weekend dad. He hated that, and in the end that was what he'd ended up being.

It was growing dark when Savannah let herself into the suite. Jacey was watching television and Declan was again at the computer. He looked up, relieved to see her. He hadn't been worried, precisely. But had wondered all evening where she was.

"Have a nice time?" he asked.

Jacey looked at her.

"Where did you go?"

He wanted to hug her for asking the question that was at the forefront of his mind.

"Sightseeing. Then I had dinner at a fabulous Chinese restaurant. Did you enjoy the cable-car ride?"

Jacey nodded. "I got to stand on the platform. It was cool."

Declan wanted to know where Savannah had been. Had she been with someone she knew, or had she gone sightseeing alone? He looked back at his computer. He regretted no longer having the right to ask.

"The laundry sent back our clothes," Jacey said. "Dad showed me how to pack the backpack. Want me to help you?"

Savannah hid her surprise and nodded. "Sure."

The two of them headed for the room they shared. Declan watched as his daughter displayed more energy than she had the entire time she'd been staying with him. He hoped she'd continue going back to being the lively, happy child he so longed for.

But it was his awareness of Savannah that had him staring at the open doorway for so long. It had started in New York and wouldn't let go.

He wished she'd gone with them today. She would have made the excursion even more fun and given him time with her—precious minutes that he'd never expected to have.

\* \* \*

"So riding the cable cars was fun," Savannah said as she folded her shirts and then rolled them to stuff in the backpack.

"I had a good time," Jacey said, sitting yoga-fashion on her bed watching. "Did you ride them?"

"I did."

"Maybe the trip won't be so bad," Jacey said thoughtfully.

"Your dad just wants to make you happy," Savannah said. If only Jacey knew how much the man had tried to make her happy would her attitude soften a little?

"I guess. Did your dad want to make you happy?"

"He died before I could remember him."

"Oh." The teenager was silent for a moment. "That must have been tough."

"Both my parents died before I was four. My sister and I went to stay with our grandmother."

"What was that like?"

"We didn't have much. Grams was old when Stacey and I went to live with her. She had arthritis pretty bad, too. But she did her best for us. And I had my sister. While we lacked material things, we never lacked love. Grams died shortly after I left for college. Stacey and I often think she held on until we were out of the nest."

"Oh."

"Cherish your parents, Jacey. You don't know how long you'll have them," Savannah said lightly. She didn't want to scare the child, but maybe she needed a nudge to begin to appreciate what she did have.

"Dad said we'll get the rest of the supplies and pick up the car in the morning. We'll leave around nine. It'll take several hours to get to the trailhead where we're leaving the car," Jacey said. "I called Mom again, but she didn't answer."

"What were her plans for the summer?" Savannah asked.

"Spend it with friends," Jacey mumbled, pulling out her phone and looking at it.

"Nice for her to have a break, don't you think?"

"From me?" Jacey looked up sharply at that.

"From watching out for you, making sure you're safe, growing, learning. Being a parent isn't an easy job. Working as a nanny, I know exactly what parents have to do to raise children. Everyone needs a carefree break now and then."

"Normally she doesn't," Jacey said slowly. "I wanted her and my dad to get married again. I don't think Dad will. They fought a lot before they got divorced."

Savannah had seen this hope with other children she'd watched who were living with one or the other divorced parent. "I understand. Truly I do. However, did you ever have any indication your dad wanted to marry your mother again?"

Jacey shook her head. "But Mom says she never should have divorced him. They struggled all the time and then when she was gone, he became a millionaire. She wants to get married again."

"Money's not the best reason to marry someone," Savannah said, hoping she could say the right words. "Love, respect, enjoying being with the other person, those count more. Not everyone's a millionaire. If people only married millionaires, there wouldn't be many people left on the earth."

"I think he loves her," Jacey said. "She told me he doesn't date much. Doesn't that sound like he wishes he was with her?"

"No. You'll only keep yourself unhappy if you

think like that. What they had sounds like it was over a long time ago."

"I wish we were back in New York," the girl said, but less vehemently than before.

"We will be soon enough. There, I've squeezed everything in, including my mousse." Savannah lifted the backpack and was surprised at the weight.

Jacey giggled. "They're heavy, aren't they? I don't know how I'm going to manage and I'm used to heavy schoolbooks."

"We'll get used to it, I'm sure." Savannah shrugged into her backpack, fastened the strap in front and walked around a little. "Not too bad."

She took it off and looked at Jacey. "Dibs on the first use of the bathroom."

Jacey nodded and leaned back on her pillows.

It was a long time before Savannah fell asleep. She had only hours left to decide to stay or go. So far she'd not rocked the boat by even mentioning she was still considering letting the two of them go on their trek together. If Declan really wanted to bond with his daughter, it would easier if it were the two of them.

Yet she could already see the change in Jacey. Maybe his plan was working. And if she could help, she wanted to. When she'd first left Declan's office after that initial interview, she'd expected to resent Jacey. She was the reason Declan had broken off their relationship. At first she didn't warm to the child, but the past day or two had shown her how delightful the girl could be.

Or was it that she was still aware of Declan and didn't know how she would keep from falling in love with him again if they stuck close? He hadn't changed that much. Yet she refused to let herself be caught up in some silly daydreams. He'd proven once that she took second place to his daughter. If she let herself go for even a second, she would likely bring only more heartache on herself.

Being around him was like slow torture. She remembered ever touch, caress, special look. Savannah hoped she wouldn't fool herself into thinking he'd changed. That he'd ever put anyone ahead of Jacey.

She was never going to get to sleep thinking about him. She threw on her robe and went to the lounge.

They were leaving their city clothes in the car when they parked at the trailhead. If she went with them, it would be jeans and T-shirts and sleeping in sleeping bags. No amenities, no comforts. Just roughing it on the trail, man against nature.

"Like the pioneers," she said softly as she switched on a lamp and lifted the phone receiver to call room service for some warm milk. She'd do okay. She'd been raised without much comfort or modern conveniences. They'd made do. She could do it again if needed.

She stood at the window overlooking the city while she waited for the milk to be delivered. The lights sparkled. Tendrils of fog drifted by, hiding then revealing the buildings in front of her. Few cars traveled the street. She saw no pedestrians. Glancing at the clock on the shelf she saw it was almost three o'clock. No wonder it looked almost deserted outside. Everyone was asleep. Was she the only person awake at this hour?

When the discreet knock came at the door, she answered it, signing the chit and taking the tray with a solitary glass of warmed milk. Taking off the cover they'd placed on it, she saw it had a sprinkling of cinnamon.

Declan's door opened and he stepped into the lounge as she was taking her first sip.

"I thought I heard something," he said. He wore only pajama bottoms, no top. And Savannah let her gaze feast on his strong solid chest, the glass poised halfway to her mouth. He looked amazing. She remembered running her hands all over that chest, feeling the warmth of his skin, the strength of his muscles. Being held against him as they danced. Crushed against him in passion. Snuggling against him as they watched favorite television shows.

Dragging her gaze away was an effort she almost couldn't handle.

"I, um, couldn't sleep, so I thought warm milk might help," she said, moving back toward the window.

"Is Jacey giving you trouble?" he asked, standing by the open door to his bedroom. When Savannah glanced over at him, she could see the rumpled bed behind him. She quickly looked back out the window. It was safer than letting her mind go down memory lane.

"No. In fact, I'm a bit surprised at how cordial she was when I got in this evening."

"I haven't said anything, nor have you. Will you be continuing on the trip?"

Decision time. She hesitated a moment, trying to find some reason to leave, wanting just a little more time with him before saying goodbye.

"I guess I'll go," she said, taking another sip of milk.

"Good."

She didn't hear anything and thought maybe he'd returned to his room. She turned and almost spilled the milk. He was only inches away, his dark eyes gazing down at her.

"Remember when—"

"No, don't. The past is past. Let's not drag it up," she said quickly. If he only knew. Since seeing him last week she'd done nothing but drag up the past. "If I go, same rules apply. No talking about the past."

"Will you ever forgive me?" he asked slowly, reaching out to feather his fingertips over her short hair. After her shower, she had not moussed it.

"It doesn't matter if I do or don't," she said,

gripping her glass so tightly she was afraid it might break.

"I was wrong, you know. It didn't work. I should have made other arrangements. Margo and I married too young and it didn't work then. I don't know why I thought it would a second time around," he said, his eyes beseeching.

She stepped back before she could drop the glass and throw herself into his arms, begging him to kiss her the way he used to.

"I understand why you went back to her. But you had to have known before you told me…you had been seeing her, right?"

He nodded. "But only with Jacey. She seemed to dote on our daughter. And she seemed older and wiser. It wasn't until after we remarried that she showed more of her true colors. I wanted to believe her so she and I could provide a good home life for Jacey. Only Margo's agenda wasn't the same as mine."

"Some things are only discovered when proven." She turned and walked back to her bedroom. "I'm sorry things didn't work out for you the way you wanted," she said softly, and closed the door. Leaning against it she let her eyes adjust to the lack of light. Once the ambient light from the street filtered through the drapes, she made her way to her bed. Sitting on the side, she sipped the milk, wishing with all her heart that things had been different. As her grandmother had often said, if wishes were horses, beggars would ride. Wishing never changed a thing.

Life moved on. She was sadder than that happy young college girl, but wiser and more prudent. Declan Murdock was nothing but heartache, and she had learned to avoid that state.

The drive from San Francisco to where they'd leave the car at Yosemite National Park took several hours. Declan had Jacey sit in the front to navigate. For several hours Savannah watched as they talked. Gradually she was seeing the Jacey Declan wanted back. It had not been a vain dream to make a family with his daughter. With another mother, they might have succeeded. But then, if Margo had been a different woman, he might not have divorced the first time and he never would have found Savannah.

She'd never had a long-term boy friend after Declan. First she was focused on her studies in school, and she nursed her heartache. Once Vacation Nannies took off, she was gone more than she was home. Which definitely didn't help in the relationship department.

So to be cherished as Declan had once seemed to cherish her was a pipe dream. It had been fun to be part of a couple. They'd planned activities together, spent their free time doing things both enjoyed, and, she'd thought, built a stronger relationship for the future.

All the more devastating when he'd told her goodbye.

She refused to look too far into the future. She enjoyed her life. She loved children and appreciated the opportunity to explore the world. She'd seen some places others only dream about. There were still a myriad of other exotic vacation spots she'd like to visit.

Was it odd she'd never thought about getting married and having a family? Had Declan derailed that dream? Or was it just natural hesitancy because of her parents? She knew her parents hadn't planned to die so young. Life was uncertain. If something happened to her today, at least there'd be no one whose life she'd alter.

Stacey would grieve but move on. She'd not leave some child or children behind bewildered by the change in the family, raised in an environment totally different from their early years.

Savannah realized they'd been traveling in silence for a while when Jacey said,

"I'm bored." As if it were the worst of fates.

"So listen to your radio," her father suggested.

"There's no reception here. No phone reception either or I could call Mom."

Declan glanced at Savannah in the rearview mirror. He had not told Jacey yet that there would be no phone service where they were going. Savannah shrugged. Time would let the teen know. No point in saying anything. She'd support his decision. For the next couple of weeks she was his employee. And she believed in absolute loyalty.

"Want to play a game?" Savannah asked. As a seasoned nanny, she knew kids of all ages got bored on long car trips. She had several car games in her tote.

"Like what?"

"There are tons of games for car play. We can play car bingo—I have some cards with things like signs or state license plates and the first one to get all in a row wins. Or we can spot license plates and the first one to read all fifty wins."

"Like all cars from all fifty states are going to be around here," Jacey said.

"You never know. California is a very popular state. I have some Mad-Lib cards. Or how about Truth or Dare?"

"What's that?"

"Whoever goes first asks the next person a question. That person then has to say truth or dare. If truth, he or she has to answer whatever question you ask. If they say dare, you have to dare them to do something."

"Like what?"

"Like crow like a rooster."

Jacey giggled and turned to look at her. Savannah smiled back. "Want to try?"

"Okay, if I get to go first."

"Go for it."

"Dad, truth or dare?"

"Truth."

"Why did we come on this dumb trip?"

"Truth—I wanted to reconnect with my little girl."

"Oh, brother," Jacey said.

"Okay, my turn," Declan said. "Savannah, truth or dare?"

She looked at him consideringly. "Okay, truth."

"What's your favorite memory?"

"Easy, lying on the bank of the river near home watching the stars at night with my sister and Grams. She knew all the constellations and told us God knows the name of every star. I couldn't fully understand at the time, but I remember I thought that was awesome."

"Okay, your turn," Declan said.

"Jacey, truth or dare."

"Truth."

"What's your favorite memory?" Savannah asked.

There was silence for a moment.

Declan glanced at his daughter. She stared out the window.

"My daddy tucking me into bed," she said in a low voice, looking away.

He felt the clutch of emotion grab hold and threaten to strangle him.

"Dad, what's yours?"

"Like Savannah said, easy. The day you and

I went to the zoo for the first time. Actually I have a bunch of favorite memories all centering around you but that's my very favorite. I had a daughter I'd just found out about. Nothing is more special than that."

"This is a mushy game," Jacey said. "Can we play bingo?"

Savannah pulled out the cards and soon she and Jacey were deep into trying to outdo the other. Declan had to drive, so he was excused from the game. When Jacey gave a shout of triumph, he smiled. She was as excited as if she'd won something big.

The games were a hit and Jacey didn't complain about being bored the rest of the trip.

It was midafternoon when they reached the ranger station where they'd get their permit and leave their car. From now on, it was backpacking the High Sierras.

When they were loaded up and ready to go, Jacey complained her backpack was heavy.

"Each of us brings our own stuff. In addition, I'm carrying the tent and the cookstove, so I have the heavier load," Declan said, anxious to get started. He hoped to reach one of the recommended camping sites before it got too dark to set up.

"I bet Savannah's is lighter."

"I'll switch," Savannah said, taking hers off and holding it out to Jacey. The teen studied the backpack for a moment, then took hers off and handed it to Savannah. She almost dropped Savannah's and her eyes widened. "Wait, this is much heavier than mine. You're shorter than me, how can you carry all that?"

"It's my stuff, I've told you before, I'm responsible for me."

Jacey took her own pack back and put it on. "Ready," she said to her father. She opened her cell. "No bars. How am I going to charge it during the trip?"

"No electricity until we get back," her father said.

"And no bars," Savannah said.

Jacey looked up, horrified. "How can I call my mom? What about my friends?"

"We're going into the wilderness like people have done for years. You can live without your phone for a week or two," her dad said, starting off.

Savannah followed, keeping an ear out to make sure Jacey followed. They had gone several yards before the teen scrambled behind them to catch up.

"That's so unfair. I have a life, you know."

"This is life. Seeing the beauty of nature, learning how we can be one with it. Living off the grid," her father said.

"Oh, brother," Jacey said.

They reached the site Declan wanted before full dusk. Quickly he directed each of them in setting up the camp. When he unloaded the tent, Jacey complained how small it was.

"It's just to keep the dew off us and provide some shelter from the cold. It's not the Hilton," he said. "But I want to see how easy it is to set up. I know the basics, so you two follow the directions and see if you can do it. That's part of the trip, to try out this new gear."

Savannah looked at Jacey. "Now we know the real reason we're here, to wait on your father."

Jacey giggled. "Only if we can figure out how to set up the tent."

Savannah walked over and leaned closer.

"Maybe we can figure out how to have part of it collapse on him tonight."

Jacey giggled again.

Declan smiled, turning away so she wouldn't see. Trust Savannah to know how to get the girl in a better frame of mind. He knew now what the Spencers had been talking about. Vacation Nannies did have top-notch nannies. He felt proud of her success. And of knowing he'd been in on the early planning stage.

Amidst much arguing and constantly checking the directions, Savannah and Jacey had the tent erected in less than thirty minutes.

"Ta da," Jacey said when it was up.

"Great job, only the manufacturer thought it should go up in ten," Declan said.

"We'll be faster tomorrow," Savannah promised.

"Now what, oh slave driver?" Jacey asked, sitting on the ground and looking up at her father.

Declan directed the rest of the camp setup. Each followed his directions. Soon Savannah had some water boiling on the fire. The freshwater creek was cold and beautiful. Due to parasites in the water, however, it had to be boiled to be potable. Once the water was deemed safe, she put in the dried ingredients to make a savory stew.

Jacey said little once she finished laying out all the sleeping bags and throwing a rope over a limb of a tree for hoisting their provisions later to keep them safe from bears.

When she finished, she sat on the ground near the fire staring at the flames.

Savannah would give a lot to know what was going through the child's mind. Despite the fun they'd had setting up the tent, she wasn't sure Jacey had decided to enjoy herself. Working, activity, that was no threat. But introspection wasn't her thing and the silence seemed to bother her.

By the time dinner was finished, it was full dark. They washed the plates, banked the fire and prepared for bed.

Once ready for bed, the three of them sat on the ground cloth next to the small fire. It was peaceful. The night sky was full of sparkling stars. The moon was low on the horizon. The setting was silent except for the low murmur of the nearby stream.

"So can you tell us constellations or have you forgotten them?" Declan asked Savannah.

"Oh, we never forget things our Grams taught us. She'd make us learn it." She pointed out the Big and Little Dippers, and several other constellations.

"They're just stars that don't look like anything," Jacey said.

"I have a hard time envisioning the figures they are supposed to represent. Except for Leo and Orion," Savannah said. "They're so clear up here, however. In New York, there's too much ambient light to see any but the brightest stars. There's the Milky Way."

Savannah indicated several other constellations, then stopped. "You'll never remember them all," she said.

"No, but it's fun to have them pointed out," Declan said.

"There's nothing else to do up here. I can't get cell service, don't have a flush toilet or anything," Jacey said. "What's that one over there?"

The flickering fire was small, giving little warmth. Savannah shivered. It had grown colder ever since the sun had set.

"I'm getting cold," she said. "I think I'm going to get into my sleeping bag."

Grateful Declan had known what to get for the trip, Savannah got into her down sleeping bag a few moments later. In only seconds she grew warmer. Snuggling down, she let herself relax. Let father and daughter have time alone. She was tired and glad to get to bed early and be alone for a little while even if she could hear every sound within fifty feet.

Her solitude didn't last. In less than five minutes Jacey followed her into the tent and scrambled into her sleeping bag, turning her back on Savannah. A moment later Declan banked the fire and joined them.

Once in their respective sleeping bags, the tent zipped closed, Declan questioned the wisdom of his sleeping arrangement. Why had he thought it a good idea to be in a confined space with Savannah? He could smell her scent, the sweet floral fragrance that seemed so much a part of her.

She'd made it perfectly clear last night she was not interested in him. The job was solely for Jacey. Still, he wished she'd stayed up and Jacey had gone to bed early. He'd welcome some calm adult conversation. And even some insights from a professional on how to continue to get better acquainted with his daughter.

She'd given him such a sweet smile during the hike that had encouraged him, made him glad he was doing this when Jacey had him doubting every move. She was happy in the trek, that was all. He wished it had held special meaning.

Yet his goal remained steadfast. He wanted his daughter back. Surely the child of younger years was there, waiting to come out again to be the joy of his life.

Declan turned and looked at Savannah. There was little light in the tent. The fire had been banked. The only illumination came from the moon, climbing in the sky. The back of her head was toward him. Her hair was still spiky. He looked forward to the morning to see how she fared. Had she been teasing about always carrying her mousse? Or did she really fix her hair every day?

He liked it that way, it was sassy, just like he remembered her.

He'd liked it longer, too. When he could run his fingers through the softness, let the strands drift through. The sweet smell had permeated every bit of her—including her silky hair.

He'd missed her.

The next morning—more complaints. Jacey didn't have a mirror to use for her makeup. She didn't have a place to take a shower. She was cold and wanted to go home. Had she known there would be no cell service she never would have come.

"After breakfast, we'll heat some water to wash in. You don't need makeup here, there's no one around to see you. And we'll go home when our trip is finished. Time enough then to call or text your friends," he said, barely holding on to his temper. One step forward, two back. Or at least it seemed like it.

"Where are we going?" Jacey asked.

"Up the trail. We're not on a schedule. We'll stop when we want, push forward when we want. There're several overnight stopping areas along the route we're taking today, we can choose wherever we want to stop."

She grumbled again. Savannah listened with

some amusement as Declan tried to reason with his daughter.

He found he was best to change his focus to Savannah. He engaged her in conversation and she didn't like it. She was trying to keep a distance, but she sensed the genuine interest he had and that made it easier to tell him—them—more about the operations of Vacation Nannies.

She remembered their long talks into the night when he'd shared his business knowledge with her. She'd taken all the suggestions and applied them to their start-up company. When they paid off, she had so many times wished she could have shared that with him. Here was the perfect opportunity for payback.

"So then we tried the office in a prestigious location. And business doubled almost overnight."

He nodded, his eyes holding hers. The silent "Well done" warmed her heart.

Breaking eye contact she looked at her plate of reconstituted scrambled eggs. She was grateful, but the gratitude was mixed with sadness.

Once they'd cleaned up, Declan had Savannah and Jacey break down the tent, as further testing. He took notes on the things they complained about to see if he could find a way around difficulties in the instructions. Or where they weren't clear.

They started out on the trail. Tall evergreen trees flanked both sides. The air was cooler than yesterday, perfect for hiking. The sun shone in a cloudless sky and once or twice she heard the screech of an eagle. Looking up, she saw a magnificent bird floating on thermals, wings widespread.

Despite the awkwardness of dealing with Declan, Savannah was glad she'd accepted this job. The scenery was spectacular, the air so clean and fragrant with pine and cedar. She glanced at Declan once or twice. He seemed in his element here. His hiking clothes were worn in spots, like a well-loved pair of cargo pants that had seen many hikes. How did he stand being cooped up inside during the year when he could be here, exploring one of the scenic wonders of the world?

That was another aspect of her job she liked. So often families had some kind of back-to-nature adventure for vacation—whether at the beach, hiking or at a destination resort that catered with water, sun and fun. She would not like to be an office worker.

As the morning progressed, Savannah tried remembering all she could about her adolescent psychology classes. She wished she could find the key to getting Jacey to drop the act and be herself. She suspected from some of the comments the girl made from time to time that she had a great sense of humor and could even be nice. But only if she'd lose the chip on her shoulder. Normally Savannah could relate with teens quickly. Was this more difficult because of the divorce, or because of her feelings for Jacey's father?

The day grew warmer as they hiked along the narrow trail. The higher they climbed, the cooler the air was. Pockets of snow still dotted the landscape in shady sections. Wildflowers pushed up through the damp soil, yellow, blue and red. In the distance snowcapped peaks rose.

Declan had started their trek with a fast pace, but soon slowed to accommodate Savannah and his daughter. As they climbed, Jacey lagged behind, dragging her feet and scowling as she looked only at the ground immediately in front of her toes.

When Declan and Savannah stopped, Jacey almost ran into Savannah.

She looked up. Declan pointed to his left. Silently she turned to see a small herd of deer grazing in a meadow about fifty yards away. The three of them watched in silence for long moments; the deer didn't seem to notice they were sharing the area with them. Two small fawns jumped around, then went to stand near two does.

"They're adorable," Savannah said softly, the delight showing on her face. This alone made the assignment worthwhile. She was enchanted.

Declan glanced beyond her to Jacey. She seemed equally enthralled. Miracle of miracles, there was a smile on her face.

Another group of hikers could be heard coming up behind them. They were laughing and talking. The deer lifted their heads, then in the blink of an eye bounded into the grove of trees beyond and vanished.

"Oh," Jacey said, turning to look behind her with a scowl.

Three couples came into view. They seemed

completely oblivious to the scenery surrounding them, too intent on their conversations.

"Hi," they said as they drew closer, glancing around. "Is there something to see from here?"

"Just taking a breather," Declan said easily. "Great day, isn't it?"

"Sure is. Enjoy." They passed and continued with their talk and laughter.

"They're going to miss a lot being so noisy," Jacey said. "I wish they hadn't scared the deer."

"We'll see more—if we let them get far enough ahead of us," Declan said.

"Until then, we can spot wildflowers," Savannah said. "I brought a chart of Sierra wild-flowers. It's rolled up in my backpack, can you get it, Jacey?"

"Geez, are you sure you aren't a teacher?" Jacey grumbled, but she reached into Savannah's backpack as instructed.

"I'm sure. I think it's fun to learn new things. I've never been here before, and who knows if I'll ever come back. I want to enjoy everything today I can."

Jacey blew out a breath as she pulled out the laminated chart. The three of them looked at it when Savannah unrolled it, then looked at some of the flowers growing in the meadow.

"Okay. The flowers are sort of pretty," Jacey said.

Declan had to hand it to Savannah, she was making headway. He was grateful for that.

The rest of the day was actually enjoyable. Jacey and Savannah began a contest to see who could spot a new flower. They checked each one that could compare with the chart Savannah had. Stepping off the trail at one point, Jacey's foot got covered with water and mud. The snow melt made everything soggy. But instead of complaining, she just shook off the water and stepped back on the trail.

Savannah had Declan sharing the wildflower descriptions and tried to spot them, as well. But he spent more time watching Savannah and her genuine delight in recognizing flowers from the chart she had. She found life exciting. He wanted that for his daughter. And himself.

They passed another group of hikers going the opposite direction and had another couple pass them in midafternoon, going at a strong, fast pace.

"Now, *they're* in shape," Savannah murmured as they nodded and passed in seconds.

"But they're going too fast to see the flowers," Jacey said. "Or any deer. I wish we'd see another bunch."

"Look there," Declan said, pointing skyward. Another eagle soared above them

"Wow, is that an eagle?" Jacey asked.

Jacey stepped closer and Declan threw his arm around her shoulders, leaning down so his face was close to hers as they watched the bird.

Savannah watched the father and daughter. They looked right together. With no makeup on, Jacey looked like the young teenager she was. Her hair was still that awful flat black, but at least for a few days, she'd have a healthier look without the makeup. She hoped this would work for Declan's sake. He was trying so hard.

They picnicked with trail mix and bottled water in the shade of a huge cedar. The ground was damp, so they used a ground cloth to sit on.

"This is nice," Savannah said. "It's hard to believe people back home are hurrying to work, hurrying home from work, doing errands and all the while I'm lounging in beautiful country, enjoying myself."

"Guilt-free," Declan said.

She looked at him. "What does that mean?"

"You can't do anything here, so all the ought-to-dos are gone. You can enjoy doing nothing guilt-free."

Jacey laughed.

Savannah turned to look at her. "What are you ignoring guilt-free?" she asked, delighted to see the girl's spontaneous laughter.

"Chores around the apartment. And no homework."

"You wouldn't have homework anyway over summer."

"Yeah, but it's hard sometimes to make the switch. I find I still feel like I should be doing something about studying even after school gets out."

"Then I'll see what more I can do to help," Savannah teased.

"Hey, flowers are enough for today. At least I don't have to take a test."

Savannah pretended to be in deep thought.

"Maybe I can have a geology lesson. Talk about the mountains here."

"I'd rather learn map-reading. Dad's map is topographical, how do you know how to read that?"

Declan reached for the map in an outside pocket of his backpack. "I can show you," he said flipping it open. "It's easy once you get used to it. It shows the terrain so we know if we'll be going uphill, finding a valley or a wide meadow."

"Too bad it doesn't show where there'll be more deer," Jacey said, looking over at the map.

"We're about here," Declan said, pointing. "And we'll follow the trail here. See where it opens up for a while? That'll be a meadow."

The two studied the map for a few minutes. Then Declan suggested they move on to reach the meadow as a stopping place for the night. "There's no water there, so if we don't find a snowbank, we'll have to use what we're carrying," he said as they donned their backpacks.

"And if we find a snowbank, remember the first rule of winter—don't eat yellow snow," Jacey said.

Declan laughed. "You remembered."

"Always, how many times did you tell me that when we went to the snow in Vermont that Christmas? And you always laughed. It's not that funny."

"Maybe not, but at the time it was," Declan said a look of amusement still on his face.

Savannah looked away. It hurt to be excluded from special moments in his life. She had thought they would share them. And look where they were today.

The hike that afternoon after their lunch stop was delightful. Jacey began to talk without the attitude. Mostly with Declan, but now and then she'd say something to Savannah. By the time they stopped for dinner, Savannah was beginning to think Declan's idea was working exactly as he wanted. By the end of the hike, his sweet child would be back, and she hoped the surly teenager was gone for good.

Thinking about the end of summer reminded her she might not ever know the outcome. She was hired to be with Jacey only for this trip; the assignment ended when they returned to New York. She kept up with some families, but others were a one-time holiday, never to be heard from again.

The agency sent cards at Christmas, and she sometimes wrote a personal note to the families she'd really liked. Sometimes they asked for her again. But there were children growing up now she'd enjoyed watching a few years ago, about whom she knew nothing more. Ships passing in the night, never to see each other again.

As it would be with Declan and Jacey.

Whether discussing his business, his family or remembering happy memories, she couldn't help seeing them all through the eyes of might-have-been.

Still, she thought as she gazed around her, while her sister had an assignment on the beach in Spain, Savannah wouldn't trade this hike for anything. Painful memories and all.

# CHAPTER FIVE

ON THE fourth day, Declan woke early. The trek was going better than he'd expected. Which was fortunate. If he'd been continually subjected to Jacey's attitude as she'd so charmingly displayed it when she'd been left with him, he didn't know if he could have coped. He ran a multimillion-dollar company, but his daughter baffled him at every turn.

As did Savannah. It was easy to understand why she kept her distance from him. He deserved it for the way he'd treated her. He couldn't help but wonder if she'd hold that decision against his daughter. But she showed no evidence of it at all. Granted she treated him like a stranger— kept him at arm's length, but with Jacey, she was friendly and was gradually working with his daughter to build her confidence, tease her out of sulks, and show that she could have a good time despite her initial reluctance.

Today was the turning point. They'd be heading back to the car and then on their way to the resort in Taylor. Much as he was enjoying the time with his daughter, he was also anticipating discussions with the resort. Murdock Sports already had several major stores across the country. This would be a different kind of outlet—high-end clothes and gear—specialty shopping tailored for that particular resort.

He'd debated taking Jacey along when he saw how she looked these days. But since they'd arrived in California the outrageous aspect of her attire had softened. He hoped, with Savannah's help, she'd not be a detriment at the resort. If it didn't work out, he'd have them driven back to San Francisco. He thought they'd enjoy the resort and give him space to deal with the opportunity to expand.

After breakfast they packed up. Their backpacks were lighter now as the food was being consumed. No more complaints from Jacey first thing each morning. And Savannah had never given a single complaint. She still moussed her hair every day. Fascinated, he loved to watch, hoping she didn't notice.

In fact, he loved watching her do anything. From working with Jacey to setting up the tent, which they could do in under seven minutes now, to her enchantment with the wildlife they'd seen, to her sparring gently with his daughter. She had a great sense of humor and was able to draw the same from Jacey.

"Today we head back down the trail," he said, pulling on his load. "By the time we reach the car in a few days, it'll be time to move on to the resort."

"If it has a hot shower, I'm all for it," Jacey said.

"I wouldn't mind one myself," Savannah added. "I guess I thought we'd be hiking a bit longer."

"It'll take us three days to return. Then you'll get to rest."

"But you'll be working," Jacey said.

"Not all the time."

"What'll we do there?" she asked.

"There are tennis courts and swimming pools, hiking trails. And a day spa—maybe you and Savannah would like that."

"No maybe about it, that's right up my alley," Savannah said.

"What's a day spa?" Jacey asked.

"You'll love it. You get to be pampered all day—massages, manicures and pedicures, hair styled—though I like mine the way it is," Savannah said.

Declan looked at her. "I do, too."

She looked at him in astonishment.

Jacey looked at her. "Would I have to get my hair styled?"

"You don't have to do anything. It's usually buffet style—you pick and choose the aspects you want. They do makeovers which are really fun. I'm sold."

Instead of the scowl Declan expected, Jacey looked thoughtful.

They retraced their steps, seeing the scenery a second time from the opposite direction. Once they saw a mother bear and a cub at a distance. Declan had them go quietly so the bears wouldn't notice three hikers. But Jacey and Savannah insisted they stop for a moment to watch the cub's antics. When Jacey laughed aloud, he hurried them along.

He had enjoyed the trek more than expected. Even with Savannah. He wished he could turn the clock back.

* * *

It seemed to Savannah as if the next days passed in double time. They were familiar with the terrain and better suited to walking long stretches than they had been when they started. They saw more wildlife on their way and passed more hikers as the weather was warming and people were taking advantage of the open trail.

Declan gradually shifted his own focus from testing the new hiking gear to the business opportunity ahead. He spent less time in conversation. Twice she saw him lost in thought when his daughter asked a question. She'd call his name loudly before he'd react.

The day before they were to reach the car it rained. A sudden storm came upon them before they knew it. Declan quickly erected the tent and the three of them and their backpacks huddled together inside as the rain poured down.

"This'll melt the snow," he said. The temperature had dropped; the dampness in the air made it seem even colder.

"We weren't walking in the snow," Savannah reminded him. She lay down on the ground cloth, using her backpack as a pillow. "I guess we were lucky we didn't have rain before."

"The forecast didn't call for it when we left San Francisco," Declan said. "But maybe it's just a local storm. Quickly started, quickly over."

"Or maybe it'll rain until tomorrow and we can't even cook dinner," Jacey said, gloomily.

"We have trail mix."

"For dinner?" The horror in her voice had Savannah smiling again.

"Think of this as an adventure. Won't it be fun to tell your friends when you get back?"

"None of them will care a bit about my summer vacation. They're doing cool stuff like exploring New York or going to Coney Island or the Hamptons."

"Ummm," Savannah said, looking at Declan. In such close quarters it was hard not to. So maybe neither of the others would suspect she looked at him when she could, when he was not watching her. It make her heart race and gave her squishy feelings inside. Determined to ignore the sensations, she listened to the rain and wondered if she could get Jacey to have a makeover. And new hairstyle.

Their last night camping, and they were stuck in the tent. When Declan excused himself to "use the facilities," as he said, Jacey looked at Savannah. "I wish we weren't going to this resort after all," she said softly.

"Because?"

"Dad's not the same. When we were hiking today he didn't see the deer until I pointed them out and I had to call him twice."

"I'm sure he's thinking about business."

"What about me?"

"What about you? He hasn't forgotten you. He's taking you on this great trip. And I expect you'll love the resort."

"But he won't be with us, I bet. He'll be all business. Like he is at home."

"It takes a lot to run a successful company like your dad's," Savannah said. She'd seen the change in Declan as well and hoped once he was at the resort he'd remember to spend time with Jacey. "Try getting him to talk about it. After all, you have a good shot at being the president of that company someday."

Jacey looked at her in surprise. "Me?" she squeaked.

"You're his only heir. Who else is he leaving everything to?"

The teenager was silent for a moment. Then she shrugged. "He could get married again and have more kids."

"Still, he adores you. Even if he has other children in the future, you'll always be his first-born precious child. And if he has a boy, what's to say the boy would want to work in sporting goods? He might want to be a soldier or a banker or artist."

"I don't know if I want to work in sporting goods," Jacey said thoughtfully.

"So find out about the business, see if it's something you'd be interested in. Get him talking—he'll love that you're interested, even if in the future you decide to do something else," Savannah said.

Declan came back shaking the rain off himself as much as he could before sitting down and looking at the two of them sitting so close. "What's up?"

"The moon," Jacey said, then laughed.

"The stars," Savannah said and smiled at Jacey.

"The rain clouds." The teenager laughed again. "So, Dad, tell me about the boutique at the resort."

If Declan was surprised at the question coming out of the blue he didn't show it. He relayed a brief version of what he planned to propose and what he was looking to find out on their visit. Savannah was pleased at some of the questions Jacey asked. They showed genuine interest—perhaps for the first time. When they turned in that night, Savannah also knew much more than she had before. Quietly, in the dark, with only the gentle sound of the rain for background, Jacey asked more questions.

Savannah liked listening to Declan talk. His thoughtful approach to the opportunity reminded her of his warnings and guidance when she was in class. Not for Declan the exciting pie-in-the-sky outlook. He was a firm businessman wanting to make sure his business ran efficiently and profitably. She remembered the discussions they'd had in the class she'd attended. Some of his ideas flew in the face of long-established traditional business models. Yet he was now living proof his ideas worked.

As they had worked with Vacation Nannies.

Savannah listened to Jacey and her father talk and felt a twinge of envy. She didn't remember her parents. Grams was the only family she'd known except for her sister. How often had she longed as a child to have the normal family unit of parents and kids? Too numerous to count. She wished Jacey would appreciate what she had. Even with her parents divorced, she still had the love from both, and she could spend time with them.

"It's getting late. I'm going to sleep," Savannah said. They had unpacked in the limited space and spread their sleeping bags.

"Dad and I'll stay up. We're talking," Jacey said proudly.

Savanna hid a smile. Gone, for now, was the attitude. There was hope for the teen.

"We'll be quiet soon," Declan said.

"I'm so tired, I won't even notice," she said. Savannah fell asleep listening to the murmur of Declan's voice, a smile on her face and an ache in her heart.

The next morning they awoke to a cloudless day. Everything dripped from the rain, but the tent had kept them dry. After a hasty breakfast, they were on their way. They'd reach the car by midday, drive to the resort and be there in time for dinner. During the walk, Declan fell into step with Savannah.

"What caused Jacey's interest last night?" he asked.

"Shouldn't your daughter be interested in what you do?" she asked, glancing over her shoulder to glimpse Jacey studying the trees they were walking through.

"Never happened before," he said.

"Just be glad she's interested."

"I am, just wondering what brought about the change. Are you glad to be going to the resort?"

"In some ways, of course, but I think this hiking idea was good. Look how much she's changed in such a short time. A few more days and she might even want to change her hair back."

He laughed softly. "Wish that was so." He smiled at her. "I appreciate your hanging in there. She's still snippy but definitely improving."

Jacey caught up with them. "I hope we see some more deer before we reach the car," she said, from her dad's left. Savannah was on his right but dropped behind them as they walked.

"Me, too. But we always have the memory of that first day," Declan said.

"We should have brought a camera. I could take pictures to send Mom," Jacey said, head up, looking around.

Declan nodded. "We can get a disposable one at the resort and take some picture there."

"But we missed those deer," she said.

"We'll take others. That image you'll have in your head anytime you want to think about it," he said. Declan was pleased with the change in Jacey in just a few short days. Granted she still lapsed into sulky behavior. She hadn't exactly warmed up to Savannah, but they interacted in a way that was good for his daughter. With the heavy makeup gone she looked much more like the sweet little girl he remembered.

He glanced at Savannah. Opportunity lost. He wished the two of them had been on the trek alone. Spending nights together in the tent. Seeing the splendor of the mountains, the soaring eagles together. Sharing.

Even with the distance she kept, he wished they had a few more days in the wilderness. He knew once they reached the resort his free time would be limited.

Savannah looked up at the sky and smiled. He felt it like a fist to the chest. He wanted one of those smiles directed toward him.

He scanned the trail ahead. How soon would they reach the car? The sooner they were at the resort, the sooner he could get to work and avoid so much time with her.

He had dated occasionally over the years since he and Margo had split the second time. Not often, and not for long. More time was devoted to building the firm. Now he could coast a little—but that didn't mean he wanted to get entangled with some woman. None had compared with Savannah in making him feel like the most important man in the world.

Frowning, he focused on the immediate future, getting to the resort, checking in with the New York office, starting the ball rolling with the potential negotiations. He needed to let go of all thoughts of Savannah. He hoped he could.

They arrived at the resort around four o'clock. Once again they had a suite, but this one had three bedrooms. Declan showered, shaved and dressed in casual clothes, pulled out the laptop and called his second in command. It was evening in New York, but Nick had been expecting his call and was still at the office.

Leaving the lounge area available for Jacey and Savannah, he settled down to business in his room, forgetting all else but the business model Nick had been working on since Declan had called from San Francisco.

Savannah didn't know the plans for dinner, so after she showered she dressed in one of her new casual hiking outfits and regular cross trainers, prepared to wander around the place and get her bearings. She'd barely noticed the amenities of the resort when they arrived, Declan had been in too much of a hurry to contact his New York office.

She wandered into the common room of the suite, wanting to explore the resort but not leaving Jacey behind. She knocked on her door. In seconds the teenager opened it. Her hair was still damp, hanging straight down her back. No makeup so far. But the black was back. Black T-shirt, black jeans, black shoes.

"Want to explore the resort?" Savannah asked.

"Where's Dad?"

"I think still in his room talking with New York, that's what he said he'd be doing. We can walk around, check out stuff and be back in time for dinner."

"I guess."

They retraced their steps to the large lobby then took one of the halls branching off that held the allure of shops. A gift shop, a clothing store, a jewelry store and a small office area opened along the hall.

"Why would someone want to buy jewelry when on vacation?" Savannah mused as she gazed into the window display with large rings, bib necklaces and assorted tennis bracelets.

"Maybe someone gets engaged here and the guy wants to buy something for her," Jacey said, also looking at the sparkly items.

"Which do you like best?" Savannah asked.

"That blue one, on the right there," Jacey responded promptly, pointing to the sapphire ring.

"That's pretty, I like that necklace," Savannah

said, pointing to a simple diamond pendant hung from a long platinum necklace.

"It's sort of plain," Jacey said.

"So's your ring."

"But chunky rings would be hard to wear and not hit against things. I'd think you'd like that necklace," Jacey pointed to an elaborate diamond and ruby bib necklace that had to be worth a fortune. "It's the one my mom would want," she finished.

"Ummm, different tastes. Come on, let's check out the clothes. I bet this is as upscale as your mom's place of work."

"Yeah, I've only been there once. She said it's not for kids."

They looked at the clothes; Savannah was slightly startled at the high prices. Fortunately, she wasn't planning to buy anything, just look. But when Jacey seemed drawn to another light blue dress, Savannah made a mental note to see if Declan would get it for her.

"Paging Savannah Williams, Savannah Williams." A uniformed hotel employee was walking down the main hall.

Savannah looked at Jacey and hurried from the shop.

"I'm Savannah Williams," she called to the man.

"A message for you." He handed her a white slip of paper with a note on it from Declan.

Where are you two? Let's get ready for dinner.

"Shopping postponed," she said with a grin to Jacey. "Your dad's hungry. We need to get ready for dinner."

Jacey walked beside her back to the elevators, eyeing the other guests as they walked along. There were families, singles, young couples and retirees—a wide assortment of ages and interests. But it seemed to Savannah that Jacey paid the most attention to the other teenagers. None of whom were dressed in black.

From a couple of sidelong glances and giggles that followed, Savannah suspected the teenagers were having a great time. She glanced at Jacey who looked at them with longing. Could she find a way to have Jacey hook up with other teens at the resort? Maybe there were special activities for that age group.

Savannah wore the same dress and sandals she'd worn in San Francisco. She'd planned more for hiking the High Sierras than dining at a fancy resort. Not that she didn't have other appropriate dresses, but only two more. This remained her favorite.

When she stepped into the lounge shortly before seven, Declan was already waiting. He wore his suit and white shirt. She saw the gleam of appreciation in his eyes and was glad she'd worn the dress again. Not that it meant anything. But every woman likes to be appreciated when she takes the time to dress up.

"Jacey and I were in one of the dress shops when you paged. I think she saw another dress she liked that wasn't black. Maybe she'll try it on tomorrow," she murmured, wishing she could just stop and stare at the gorgeous man in front of her.

"Have her charge it to the room," he said casually. "Where is she?"

"Coming. Where are we eating?"

"The Montgomerys have asked us to join them

in the Mariposa Room. I said we'd be there at seven."

"Oh, I shouldn't go then."

"Why not?"

"If it's business, I have no need to be there."

"It's not business, it's dinner. Jacey and you are included."

Savannah still wasn't sure she should attend. This assignment was as unlike any other as she'd ever had. First, she'd never been so aware of a child's father as she was of Declan. No matter how often she told herself she couldn't allow herself to trust him, it didn't stop the awareness that grew daily.

Awareness exacerbated by the memories of his touch, his kisses, his very presence in her past. Funny how she hadn't thought about him in years and suddenly it was as if they'd parted only yesterday. Every memory she had popped to the forefront of her mind and she was hard-pressed to ignore the longing that grew.

A yearning for what could never be.

"Did you get all your work done?" she asked for distraction.

"Enough. It's late back in New York and so

I sent them home. We'll get going again in the morning."

Jacey opened her door and both Savannah and Declan turned toward the door. She stepped out, looking warily at both of them, defensively, as if in challenge.

She wore the blue dress bought in San Francisco. No makeup and her dark hair was pulled back from her face and tied at her neck with a white ribbon.

"Don't you look nice. Ready to go? We'll be eating with Harry and Ada Montgomery. They own the resort, though their children run it now," Declan said.

"I'm ready. What'll we talk about?" she asked, looking back and forth between Savannah and her father.

"Business, mostly, I expect. You okay with that?" Declan asked.

"I guess." She darted another questioning look at Savannah.

"You look very nice," Savannah said with a smile.

"Thanks," she mumbled and went to the door.

"Actually, you look beautiful," Declan said as he held the door for them to pass through.

Jacey ducked her head, but Savannah saw the happy smile.

Dinner went better than Savannah had expected. Ada Montgomery was a delightful older woman who was immediately taken with Jacey. Declan had been right, Jacey had a delightful personality when she wasn't convinced she needed to make a statement designed to drive her father up the wall.

Ada was originally from New York City and spoke of the fun she'd had growing up there. Soon she and Jacey were comparing notes. Savannah was pleased that the woman drew out the teen, but was shocked when Jacey said, "I need to get my hair fixed. Does the spa here do things like that?"

"Of course, dear, we have some of the best people on the west coast. How about you and me, and Savannah, of course, do a full day tomorrow at the spa. It'd be my pleasure to treat you both. And you'll love all the pampering."

Jacey glanced at Savannah. "She said spas were wonderful."

"Ah, a wise young woman."

Jacey seemed unconvinced. "She's my nanny. Not that I need one, but Dad's old-fashioned that way."

"Ah, a properly chaperoned young lady. Nicely done by your father," Ada said wisely.

Jacey stared at her in surprise, then her expression grew thoughtful. "Yeah, I guess she is more like a chaperone. Not that I need one of those either. She's almost like an older friend."

Savannah couldn't believe her ears.

"Friends are important to have. And I also have friends of varying ages. Makes life so much more enjoyable," Ada said with a friendly smile at Savannah.

Jacey stared at her. "Really?"

"Friends are those you can confide in, too. I've been my husband's confidante for forty years. He talks with his men friends, but I know what's really important to him. We're best friends."

"You're his wife, that's your job."

"Oh, no. Many husbands and wives are not best friends," Ada said.

Jacey looked at her dad. "My mom and dad aren't friends."

"Were they once?" Ada asked.

"I don't know. I only see them arguing."

"Not best friends, then. What does your mother do?" the older woman asked, changing the topic smoothly.

The talk centered on Margo for a while. Savannah listened, picking up on some of Jacey's comments. She wondered if she should share with Declan. Jacey wasn't telling her, she was telling Ada. So no confidentiality involved. He should know what she was going through. Savannah had an idea he hadn't a clue.

After dinner they thanked the Montgomerys and returned to the suite.

"She's nice," Jacey said in the elevator. "And she's going to treat us to the spa tomorrow."

"Sounds like fun," Declan said.

When they reached the suite, Jacey went straight to her room, but Savannah stared at Declan hoping he'd pick up on not retiring immediately. He did.

Once the door closed behind his daughter, he turned to Savannah. "Want a brandy or something before we go to bed?"

"A small one. I wanted to talk to you about Jacey."

"I figured as much." He poured the brandy and brought it to one of the sofas, gesturing for Savannah to sit. He sat beside her, handed her a glass then touched his lightly to hers.

"Thanks for all you're doing," he said.

"That's why you hired me. I think you should know some of how Jacey spends her life with her mother. Alone many evenings, no one to attend school activities and a series of men in and out of their lives who may or may not be her future stepfather."

She relayed what she'd learned that evening. Declan grew more frustrated the more she revealed.

"I thought she'd be better off with her mother," he said finally, standing and pacing to the window. It was black out except for the lights on the grounds. He turned. "I've thought over the past couple of years I should ask her to live with me. Or at least spend more time with me. I want her to grow up with my values and ideals. Not only her mother's."

"Are you going to devote any more time to her than Margo does? Your business seems all-consuming," Savannah asked. "Or are you planning to have Mrs. Harris fill in full-time?"

He studied her for a moment, lost in thought.

"Balance, remember?" she said. "That was one of the tenets you pounded into our heads in the class. Don't let the business become all-consuming. At the end of the day, leave it behind, refresh and hit it hard the next day."

"I hate it when people quote things I said back to me," he grumbled.

She laughed, setting her glass on the coffee table. "Touché. Pay attention, Professor, the words hold true. More so when children are in the equation. They grow so fast. I bet it seems like yesterday she was that little seven-year-old you had just met."

He nodded, studying the last of the brandy in his glass. Tossing it back, he put the empty glass on the windowsill.

"I don't want her to exchange one neglectful family situation for another," he said. "I'll have to think about it and feel Jacey out about it, as well. There'd still be the problem of her coming home from school while I was working. Mrs. Harris would be there, but not to entertain her."

"She could entertain herself. Or, you could find her a spot at the company where she could do her homework, then ride home with you. Encourage her interest in the business. She might surprise you," Savannah suggested, sipping her brandy.

"You mean she might have a genuine interest, not just one forced on her because she was bored on the hike?"

"Exactly." Savannah rose and joined him by the window. "Don't neglect her while you work. We know you need time, but the expectation when we left New York was devoting exclusive time to recapturing the fun you had camping and hiking when she was younger. You need to make sure she knows she still has your full attention when she needs it."

He reached for her hand, lifted it to his lips and kissed it. "You're amazingly astute about children. You've changed over the years."

Savannah stared at her hand in his, feeling the tingling down to her toes. She refused to meet his eyes, afraid of her own weakness. She wanted to draw him closer, kiss him, hold him. To forget for a little while that they were no longer strangers.

"Not necessarily. These are my suggestions, who knows what's going to work with her?"

Her focus wouldn't move from Declan, on the hand that held hers, on the warmth on the back of her hand that had been kissed. Chancing it, she looked up. His eyes gazed into hers.

"Want to take a walk?" he asked slowly.

"Where?"

"Outside. I miss the night sky, the freedom we had on the trail."

"It'll be cold out."

"Get a jacket."

"Oh, won't that look nice with this dress."

"I'll give you ten minutes to change."

Savannah hesitated. She was being foolish. A prudent woman would bid him good-night and go to bed. Temptation proved too strong. She knew their time together was fleeting. Throwing caution to the wind, she decided to give in to desire for tonight.

"Deal." She whirled and hurried to her room.

Stepping outside from the lobby a few minutes later, Savannah felt as giddy as a schoolgirl with her latest crush. This was probably a stupid move, but she pushed her doubts away. She'd told Jacey they were going out for some fresh air. The teen was listening to music and didn't care.

The sweatshirt and long pants felt good in the cool mountain air. The lights around the resort blotted some of the stars, but many could still be seen overhead. They took a path away from the buildings and soon were surrounded by tall pines and firs, blocking the resort light while permitting only limited light from the stars.

"If we get lost, it's on you," she said taking a deep breath of the crisp air.

He reached for her hand. "As long as we stay on this trail and then turn around, how can we get lost? Remember when we went for a stroll at that place in the Adirondacks? There'd been no moon that night."

"But we had flashlights. I remember Stacey and I used to sneak out of Grams' house some nights to go on fishing trips with some of the kids from school. We thought at the time no one knew, but now I suspect every detail was known, but deemed safe enough. Palmerville, West Virginia, isn't exactly a hotbed of crime. Or anything else for that matter. It was always a little spooky in the dark. I was younger then, of course."

"So you'd go to the local fishing hole. Ever catch anything?"

"No. Who catches fish at night? And if we had, how would we explain that to our parents or Grams?"

"I'm sure you would have come up with something."

"Ever go night fishing?"

"No. Our greatest activity was playing softball then baseball by the time I got into high school. I hated to go home from the park as I remember. Those were great days."

"Are your parents still doing well?" Savannah had never met them. But Declan had spoken about them from time to time.

"My dad is. He lives in Albany. Married again about three years after my mom died. They're happy."

"I'm sorry. I didn't know she'd died. I bet your dad's proud of you."

"I hope so. And if so, it's more because I'm a good man than for all the money I've made. He was disappointed my marriage didn't take.

I don't think he cared that much for Margo, but he adores Jacey."

"Jacey needs as much family as she can get. To gain different perspectives. Her mother sounds like a self-centered, money-hungry woman."

"Makes you wonder, doesn't it? I'd think you'd have more reasons to crave money, coming from a poor background. Margo never had it as bad as you. Yet you have balance and she doesn't."

"I have much more than I ever had before, and actually more than we anticipated when we started Vacation Nannies. I'm living just the way I want. I have savings in the bank. What more could I want?"

"Millions?"

"Why? It'd just swell my bank account. Money for money's sake doesn't do much for me. But having enough to live like I want to does."

"You wouldn't have to work if you had millions," he suggested.

"I love my work. I adore children, and I really like visiting exotic locations."

"You could travel if you had millions."

"Like you do?" she asked, teasing. It was easier

walking in the dark to forget the past and future, to live in the moment. She was enjoying herself.

"Hey, I'm here aren't I? This is a vacation."

"Yes, selling more product to another client. Making even more money."

"You make money when you go to exotic locales," he countered.

"True, but I'm also enjoying myself. And someone else is paying for my trip, so why should I quit work to pay for my own trips?"

"You have fun with every assignment, don't you?" he asked.

"Pretty much, why would I do it if I didn't? Don't you like what you do?" she asked.

"Yes, but for the challenge, for the testing of my business acumen, not for fun."

"So, different strokes and all that. The end result is the same. We're happy."

He stopped and turned to face her. "Are you, Savannah? Really happy? I didn't mess up your life? I didn't ruin everything, did I?"

The serious question caught her by surprise. She considered it for a moment. "No one else has the ability to mess up my life. Only me. I like where I am now." She hoped that would suffice.

She didn't want to tell him how much he'd hurt her. And in the end, she did like where she was in life.

He was silent a moment, then said, "You're making a difference in my life and my daughter's and for that I thank you, Savannah. I hope by the end of the vacation she'll be happy. And maybe you'll find it in you to forgive me."

He leaned over and kissed her.

When the first instant of surprise had vanished, Savannah sank into the kiss. For a few moments she was transported to the happiest time of her life. The sensations that raced through her heated her blood and made her wish for things that could never be.

She pushed even closer, wrapping her arms around him and kissed him back. Endless moments passed. Or did time stand still?

Floating, feeling, fantasizing. Forever felt just a heartbeat away.

Then slowly, he pulled back, trying to see her in the darkness.

Her breath came fast and hard. Reality returned. She let her arms fall and stepped back.

"Do you want me to apologize?"

"Not at all." She tried to keep her voice level, free of the swirling emotions that threatened to swamp her. What was she doing? He was off-limits.

"I never forgot you," he said softly. His voice was low, caressing her. She wanted to close her eyes and savor every second of the past five minutes.

"Ready to return? Did you see there's a hot tub by the pool? It's open until midnight. Want to test it out?"

Another temptation. She almost asked if he would kiss her again. If he said yes, would she go or flee to her room wherein lay safety?

"That sounds exotic, it's cool enough we'd enjoy the heated water. But we'll probably freeze when we leave it." She decided she could be the sophisticated woman she'd become. A kiss was merely a kiss.

"We're hardy people, we can do it," he said.

She laughed, trying to enjoying his playful mood. Aware that every second drew her closer to danger. The danger of losing her heart again to this man. Every aspect of Declan Murdock appealed to her.

"I'd love to, however, since our plans were to hike the high country, I didn't bring a bathing suit."

"The hotel shops are open, I bet. Let's check at least."

His hand held hers as they hurried back. She couldn't help thinking about the kiss he'd just given. It had hit her with more emotion that she expected.

*I will not fall in love with Declan Murdock*, she repeated all the way back to the hotel. She only hoped she could keep to her vow. She knew she was tempting fate to continue to spend time with him alone. But for one night she could indulge. Their time together was fleeting. She yearned for some closure. Until then, she wanted to explore what being with Declan now would be like.

Savannah found a swimsuit at the gift shop. She also purchased a cover-up and put her clothes in the bag.

They entered the pool area a few minutes later. One man swam in the pool, two couples sat in chairs near the edge talking. No one was in the hot tub.

"Is the resort not full?" Savannah asked as she

shed her cover-up and walked to the bubbling hot tub, feeling slightly self-conscious in the suit. It had been the only one in her size in the boutique and she'd been grateful to have something. Normally she didn't even think about her employers when she took children swimming. Tonight, however, as she turned, she caught Declan's decidedly masculine appraisal. Those flutter-feelings started again. She stepped into the hot tub and sat down, the water coming to her chin. It was getting harder and harder to remember what was in the past and what was in the present.

"Mmm, this feels heavenly in the cool night air," she said.

He joined her a moment later and the water rose another notch. He rested his arms along the edge, tipped back his head and stared at the sky. "I might have to get one of these."

"And put it where?"

"Do you think the building manager would let me put it on the roof?"

"As long as it didn't crash into the apartment below, he might."

"Naw, too many other tenants would then want to use it. I like it like this—just us."

Her heart skipped a beat. She liked it with just the two of them, as well. She always had.

"Tell me more about your grandmother," he said. "And about growing up in Palmerville."

"Not a lot to tell." She thought a moment and then began to talk about her early feelings when her parents had died so unexpectedly and she and her sister had arrived at their grandmother's.

Time seemed to fly by. When the attendant came to close the pool area, Savannah was surprised it was so late. They'd discussed their respective childhoods and first impressions of New York when they'd moved there.

To her disappointment, there were no more kisses, or any hint of a move on his part while in the hot tub. Was he having regrets?

They dried off as best they could with the poolside towels. Covering up, they returned to the suite. Would he kiss her again? she wondered.

"Good night, Declan," she said, ready to retreat to her room.

"Thanks for spending the evening with me, Savannah." He brushed his lips lightly against hers.

She went to her bedroom and closed the door

quietly. Her heart raced. The kiss had her silently chanting the mantra to keep her heart whole, but the emotions that swirled through her had her dreaming things that would never be.

She was years older than that naive coed and wiser. She refused to fall again for the man. She'd met dozens of dynamic captains of industry, gone to events with high-level politicians, business-men, even with some European aristocracy. Why did this one man flood her with awareness and attraction and sensual feelings that wouldn't go away?

Declan stood in the lounge for a long moment after Savannah left. He felt he was balanced on a high wire, one misstep and he'd crash below. He'd wanted his funny, sweet Jacey back. Now he wanted Savannah—in a totally different way. She was beautiful, sexy. Did she have any idea how that spiky blond hair had him yearning to touch it, feel the softness beneath the mousse, run his fingers through it to see what happened?

Did she have any idea how much he longed for the trust and love she'd once so freely given? Had he made any progress tonight? Her kiss would likely keep him up tonight, remembering the feel of her body against his, her mouth moving against his, sending his desire off the scale.

Was there any probability of them becoming a couple again?

He turned and headed to his room. At least he knew where he stood with business. With women—it was an entirely different matter. Yet, even as he thought about his parting remarks so long ago, he wondered if he could change her mind. There wasn't another woman in the world like Savannah. Too bad he'd learned that too late.

# CHAPTER SIX

SAVANNAH woke early the next morning. After dressing, she went to take a quick walk, expecting Jacey to sleep in as late as she could. Teenagers loved to sleep to noon. To her surprise, Declan was standing by the window in the lounge looking out.

"Good morning," she said.

He turned and she caught her breath. He looked so amazing. Her heart picked up speed. She felt suddenly tongue-tied.

"Did you sleep well?" he asked.

"I did, you?"

"Short but good. I waited for you to have breakfast. I thought we could have it together."

Savannah considered the invitation. She wanted to spend more time with him. Not to rekindle anything, but because she could.

"Okay, sounds good."

"I'll leave a note for Jacey and we can go downstairs. Too cool to sit out on the terrace, I think, but we ought to be able to get a window table."

When they entered the dining room, they were quickly shown a table by the window. The breakfast was buffet style and once they filled their plates they sat down. Coffee appeared and Savannah took a sip as she looked at Declan over the rim of the cup.

"Anything special you wanted to talk about?" she asked.

"No. You enjoying the trip?"

"Very much. And I believe Jacey is, as well. She especially is looking forward to the spa day with Ada."

"Women love to be pampered," he murmured with a smile.

"Right on that. She's in for a treat. Apparently your ex-wife doesn't indulge as much as you think. Jacey didn't even know what a spa was."

"I don't know what Margo does now. Do you have any hints on keeping Jacey happy for the rest of the trip? I'd hoped we'd build a closeness like that we had when she was younger. But it's not moving as fast as I wanted."

"I think you need to give her time. It's only

been a couple of weeks. She's with her mother all the time, and it sounds as if Margo gives her a slanted view of things."

Declan took a moment to eat some of his omelet and gaze out the window, then moved his gaze to Savannah.

"I'm giving serious thought to asking Jacey to come live with me for the next few years. She's not going to be living at home for much longer. I've toyed with the idea for a while. Seeing her as she is now, I think it'd be for the better. Her mother's had her for her entire life, sharing her reluctantly lately. Once she graduates from high school, she'll be off to college and then on to life. If I ever want a chance to really get to know her, I need more time with her now."

"She's very protective of her mother. And I think she has a very biased outlook on the situation—Margo's position all the way."

"My fault. I should have made more of an effort while we were married. And then even more these past couple of years. I've enjoyed talking with her this trip, learning her take on things. I might have been able to head off some of the ideas Margo implanted. I should have insisted on every weekend I was scheduled."

"It's not too late. When you have free time in the next few days, spend it with her. She needs to know you care. I mean she needs to *really* know it, by your asking her opinion on things, getting her ideas. And one other bit of advice, don't come across as defensive. She'll be quoting her mother and you'll hear Margo in the words or tone. Don't react."

"You think I wouldn't come across cool and collected?"

She grinned and shook her head. "I think your first impulse would be to defend the situation and present your side as the only one."

"Isn't it?" he teased.

"Only in your mind," Savannah retorted.

"Ah, so I should do what? Turn my feelings and opinions aside?"

She shrugged. "I don't know, maybe role-play or something."

"You sound like a shrink. I hate role-playing."

"When did you ever go to a shrink?"

"Never, but I watch TV."

"Ah, but when you set the rules, you get to

be the hero. Anyway, it'll help her to get inside your head, and if she reacts differently from how you'd do it, you can correct her and teach her at the same time."

He nodded thoughtfully.

Savannah wasn't convinced he'd try it, but at least he hadn't laughed outright. She admitted she had difficulty seeing him in role-playing. But she recognized his sincere desire to reconnect with Jacey. And she wanted to help.

"Tell me your favorite vacation spot," he said, changing the subject.

"They're actually work places for me, vacations for my clients. I think my favorite was the cruise in Alaska. Not the children I watched, but the spectacular scenery I saw."

"The children were brats?"

Savannah laughed and then regaled him with an exaggerated story of some of the trials and adventures she'd had over the years with unruly kids or difficult parents. She kept the information vague enough that he'd never know of whom she spoke. But in retrospect some of her experiences *were* funny.

They sipped their coffee companionably when they'd finished eating.

"Has Vacation Nannies fulfilled all the expectations you had in class?" he asked.

"More, even," she said with enthusiasm. Savannah began telling him how they began each stage of development, watching to see if he was growing bored. He seemed as interested as if it were his own company. He had questions, made complimentary comments from time to time. She basked in his approval, still grateful for the information he'd so freely shared with the students in his class. She felt she and her sister had benefited tremendously because of it.

"Yours is the only company I know of that has succeeded so well. Makes me feel the time I spent was worthwhile," he said slowly.

"You never know when the others will venture forth and take the chance. In our case, we had nothing to lose because we started with nothing. Most of the students in that class were either focused on an MBA, which lends itself more to bigger corporations, or they already had jobs. It's hard to walk away from a steady paycheck to try something never done before," she said.

"Maybe."

Jacey pulled out a chair at their table and plopped down. She eyed the empty coffee cups. "If you'd finished, why didn't you come back to the room?" she asked.

"Good morning to you, too, sunshine," Declan said.

"Good morning," she mumbled, throwing a quick glance at Savannah. "Ada called and said we should meet her at ten at the spa. I didn't know when you were coming back to the room."

"I'm glad you joined us," Declan said. "Go pick out your food and come back."

"We'll sit with you while you eat," Savannah suggested.

"I'll get my plate." Jacey served herself and ate quietly while Declan and Savannah discussed some of the locales she'd worked in.

"How did you like celebrating the new year in London?" he asked.

Jacey looked up at Savannah. "You were in London at New Year's?"

Savannah nodded. "We had the best visit. We saw lots of the sights there and took day trips on the train to Salisbury and Bath. I'd love to have taken a car trip, but I didn't want to chance driving, and my employers were happy staying in London. I don't drive much in Manhattan, I sure didn't want to try the English roads."

"Did you spend Christmas there, too?" Jacey asked.

"Nope, I was in Paris for Christmas. Ooo la la!" Savannah grinned at her, noticing Declan's attention from the corner of her eye.

Declan watched his daughter's eyes light up.

"So you travel a lot?" Jacey asked.

"Wherever my clients are going. This was my first visit to Yosemite, however," Savannah said.

Jacey looked at her dad. "I like that we came here," she said, almost shyly.

Savannah felt a thrill of delight when Declan smiled broadly at his daughter. Maybe his plan would work better than he thought.

Savannah and Jacey met Ada at the spa promptly at ten. They were given a brief brochure describing the different stations offered, from massage to hairstyling, manicures, facials, makeovers and full-body wraps. There was even a gym where they could use any of the exercise machines.

They selected similar treatments, from the facials and makeovers to the manicures. Those could be done at the same time so they could visit as they were pampered. The massages were individual and they chose those first, planning to meet for their manicures, break for lunch and then have the facials and makeovers.

Savannah enjoyed spa services whenever she could. She loved the boneless way she felt during and after a massage. She took a warm soak in the hot tub after the massage thinking of her evening with Declan. In fact, her thoughts centered more and more on Declan. She enjoyed their time together, talking, learning more about each other and where they were now. It seemed as if they'd come to an unspoken truce and she liked that. Breakfast had been almost as enjoyable as his kiss last night.

Uh-oh, she'd best not dwell on that. It only caused more craving, more yearning for what would never be.

A short time later, she dressed in the robe the hotel furnished and went to have her manicure. Ada was there, Jacey not yet.

"This is a wonderful treat for Jacey," Savannah

told the older woman. "It's wonderful for me, too. Thank you!"

"My pleasure. I think it's so delightful. I admit I indulge myself a couple of times a month."

"If I worked here, I'd probably do it once a week," Savannah said. She was shown to an elevated chair with a foot rest and swing table. Ada sat next to her just as Jacey bounded in.

"Did you like it?" Savannah asked with a smile. The girl's energy was amazing.

"Wow, it's totally awesome! I never knew." She hopped up on the chair next to Ada. "I'm having a blast. Thanks, Ada. Wait until I tell my mom. I don't think she's ever been to a spa. She'd love it."

"You must invite her here," Ada said.

"I can't, we live in New York. But I bet there're spas there."

"Of course. Maybe the two of you could have a day together like this," Ada suggested.

"Awesome!"

They chatted while they were having their toenails and fingernails buffed, shaped and polished. When Jacey learned small designs could be painted on her fingernails she insisted on daisies.

"What a great idea," Ada said. "How about we all have one finger with a daisy to commemorate our day together?"

"Yes," Jacey said. "Sounds fun. Wait until my dad sees."

*Huge step,* Savannah thought.

"Did you go to a spa in London?" Jacey asked.

"No time," Savannah said.

"When were you in London?" Ada asked.

"New Year's," Jacey answered before Savannah could say a word. "She travels a lot."

"Sounds like such an exciting job. Getting to see the world."

"I specialized in adolescent behavior and education. But I can watch any age group. It was my way to earn a living and get to see the world."

"My, how interesting. How did you come to do that?" Ada asked.

"My sister and I don't come from a very wealthy background, so we tried to figure out what we could do to earn enough to live on and still see the world. Our service is unique and highly sought after, I'm proud to say. My sister and I own the agency and have a dozen other nannies working for us."

"I love seeing women own their own business," Ada said. "Of course, in my generation it wasn't as common, but now I believe woman can do almost anything they wish with a little imagination, hard work and commitment."

"Me, too," Savannah said.

"Don't you get attached to the kids and miss them when you get home?" Jacey asked.

"Most of the time. But I try to remember I'm part of their vacation experience, so I want them to have the best time and go home with happy memories. And for some families, I'm requested each year for vacation so I get to see the kids again as they're growing up."

"Have you been doing this long?"

"Almost seven years now. My sister and I have been all over. She's in Spain right now."

"So you'll be gone all summer?" Jacey asked.

Savannah smiled and nodded.

They ate a lovely lunch beside the pool. The day was warm and sunny though there were few swimming. They still had time after eating before returning to the spa. A group of teens were sitting at one table, laughing and talking. Jacey glanced over once or twice. Ada noticed. "Want an introduction?" she asked.

Jacey shook her head quickly. "No, we're only here a couple of days."

"There's a film showing tonight. You could go to that. Let me introduce Melissa to you. I know her parents well."

Savannah watched as Ada took Jacey over to the group and made introductions. The teens quickly moved to include her in their group, and before long Jacey was sitting with them and Ada returned.

"I hope that's all right. Did you want her to stay with us?" she asked as she sat down.

"I'm happy as long as she is. In fact, it might be a good thing for her to be around normal teens. I don't know if you noticed, but black is her favorite color at the moment, and she's far too young to pull it off."

"I know, but it's a stage. I'm sure you are aware of that," Ada said.

The afternoon passed swiftly with more luxury treatment. When they met at the entrance at the end of their session, Savannah smiled broadly when she saw Jacey. Her hair had been treated and looked normal, soft and pretty, with high-lights and a glossy sheen. It was shades lighter, almost brown with a hint of copper.

The light makeup was suitable to her age and enhanced her eyes.

"Wow, you look terrific. Wait until your dad sees you," Savannah said with enthusiasm.

"Oh, we have to buy at least one new outfit to go with our new looks," Ada said. "You do look lovely, Jacey. Come on, let's visit the boutique near the lobby. I have just the outfit for you in mind."

Some time later Savannah and Jacey entered the suite. Jacey looked disappointed when she didn't see her father waiting. "Oh, I thought he'd be here."

"He's meeting with the resort managers. He'll be along for dinner."

Jacey licked her lips and looked at herself in one of the large mirrors on the wall. "It's kind of hard to believe this is really me."

"Why? You're pretty. Now, with the extra added enhancement from the spa, your true beauty shows."

Jacey stared at the mirror. "I am sort of pretty, aren't I?"

Savannah came to stand beside her, studying her reflection. "Jacey, girl, you are *very* pretty, not sort of. And I bet you'll have those teenage boys tonight shoving each other to sit by you."

Jacey giggled. She looked at Savannah. "I guess you and Dad'll have the evening to yourselves."

"I guess we will," Savannah said neutrally, while her heart rate kicked up a notch. Would Declan want to spend the evening with her?

"Don't do anything I wouldn't," Jacey said audaciously.

Savannah laughed and turned away, already thinking about what she'd like to do with Declan—if this had been a true romantic relationship. If it had been seven years ago and he hadn't left her.

Declan finished the negotiations and rose to shake hands all around. The final touches would be handled by the attorneys, but it looked as if the deal had been hammered out to the satisfaction of both parties. If this worked, he'd look into offering boutique shops in other resorts. An entirely new facet to Murdock Sports, Inc.

He walked into the suite a short time later and stopped when he saw his daughter.

"Hi, Daddy," Jacey said, jumping up from the sofa where she'd been sitting with Savannah.

"Jacey?" he asked, taking in her glossy brown hair, the pretty girl he remembered from before. The sherbet-pink dress was perfect for a young teenager. What miracle had happened? Where was the sullen girl dressed in black with the look of a zombie?

She giggled and nodded. "Didn't you recognize me?"

"I almost didn't. You look fantastic."

Jacey exchanged a smile with Savannah, who winked.

Declan walked over and then walked around his daughter, noting that the hair color was almost her natural shade. The makeup was so subtle she had that freshly scrubbed girl-next-door look. And the dress—he thought it perfect on his daughter.

"Ada thought this was a perfect dress for me and I didn't want to hurt her feelings."

"It is perfect. You are now grounded to your room until you are twenty-five," Declan said, teasing.

For a second Jacey didn't get it, then she giggled again.

"That'll have to wait," Savannah said. "Jacey's been invited to join some other young people tonight for dinner and the movie the resort is showing."

"Do I know them?"

"No, but Ada does and she vouches for them," Jacey said. "I can go, can't I?"

Declan gave Savannah a questioning look.

"I see no reason why not," Savannah said. "If Ada Montgomery knows them and vouches for them, how could there be a problem?"

"Okay, then."

"Thanks, Daddy." Jacey hugged him and then did a little dance. "I'm to meet them in just a few minutes. I didn't think you'd get back in time."

"Then Savannah could have given permission," he said. He looked again at Savannah. She was wearing a dress he hadn't seen before. The mint-green dress fitted her perfectly, displaying her feminine figure to advantage. He studied her for a minute. "So this means you and I have dinner alone."

She nodded, her expression a bit wary.

The spark that arced between them had Declan wishing for more than dinner. Not that anything like that would happen while his daughter was around. But they wouldn't always be here in California. Once they returned to New York, Declan had plans to get in touch with Savannah—and not with business in mind. There were many years to catch up on, and a woman's mind to change. If he could.

He'd had a lot of time to think last night, since sleep had proved impossible. He'd made a mistake. A monumental one, granted. But if she was the woman he knew her to be, he hoped he could talk her into forgiveness, into forgetting. Into seeing what they could build together.

Jacey left in high spirits, and shortly thereafter Declan and Savannah went to one of the dining rooms that also had dancing. They were early. Service was prompt. In no time they had a window seat that gave way to the expanse of forest and distant mountains. It was growing dark and before the meal ended, they'd only have the lighting on the grounds to illuminate the view.

"It's so beautiful here," Savannah said. "I love the feeling of open space, of seeing land where no one has ever walked."

"You think no one has walked the land? We saw a lot of people on the trail. And even more here," Declan said. "What about the early explorers or before them the indigenous people?"

She waved her hand. "There's so much. Sure some of it has been crossed, but I bet there are miles and miles of untouched land, seen only from a distance."

"Do you want to be the first?"

She laughed and shook her head. "No thanks. I like looking at it, walking the trail like we did, but I don't need to be on that pristine land. It's just amazing to think about it, that's all. You have to admit there is not a square inch in Manhattan that hasn't been touched."

"True." She was a romantic. He remembered that from before.

"There's dancing later. I thought we could stay and enjoy that," Declan said as they waited for their meal. A lot would depend on her answer.

She hesitated a moment and then nodded. "Sounds like fun," she said, but her eyes didn't meet his.

He looked at her and caught one hand, his thumb rubbing softly over the back.

She looked at him then.

"I want you to enjoy the evening," he said slowly.

She nodded. "Thank you for asking. I love to dance. And I don't often get a chance, unless it's dancing around the nursery with a little kid in my arms."

Declan felt the attraction grow stronger. He had not expected this when he hired her.

"Tell me about Jacey's amazing transformation. I had hoped by summer's end, maybe, but she looks like her old self. How did you do it?" he asked.

"I wish I could claim credit, but it's all Ada. Jacey really admires the woman and hung on her every word today. Compliments made her happy, and they make her see herself in a different light."

"I don't want her to change back into the sullen teenager who showed up for the summer," he said.

"She's smart, Declan. I think it was a stage and now if things go well, she'll be happy with herself and not want to make such a shocking declaration. Especially if she gets involved in the activities the resort has for teenagers."

"I hope so."

"So how are the negotiations going?" she asked.

"Finished most of the details today. It looks good. I'll try it for a few months and if it continues to look profitable, I will think about a new branch to the company."

Savannah nodded, pleased for him, but not so happy to hear the negotiations were finalized. There really would be no reason for her to remain. He could spend time with his daughter. After almost not taking the assignment, now she didn't want to cut it short.

Looking down at her plate, she hoped the sudden realization didn't show. She couldn't help remembering how once she'd foolishly thought they might get married, have a family.

She wanted children. She wanted to tell them the old family stories her grandmother had told her. She wanted to see how their eyes would light up when they learned new things. Seeing the world through the eyes of a child was always so special. She wanted her own children to be enchanted with everything the world had to offer. And she wanted to be there to see it.

A little boy with Declan's eyes or unruly hair. Another girl to give him fits when she started dating.

"You've gone very quiet," he said.

She looked up and smiled, hoping he couldn't read anything into her expression. "Just trying to remember if I've ever had the rainbow trout before. It's quite delicious."

He accepted her explanation easily and the conversation veered into food they enjoyed. Many dishes she remembered from before. Now it seemed he'd also developed a taste for sushi.

When the small band stepped into place, Declan and Savannah had long since finished their meal and moved to the bar where they had after-dinner brandy and coffee. The music was familiar and both seemed glad to take to the dance floor for the first song. From faster songs to slower ones, Declan insisted they dance the night away. Savannah had a grand time. She truly loved to move her body in rhythm with the music. And an attentive dance partner made it all the more enticing.

Her favorites, however, were the slow songs when Declan drew her into his embrace and moved with the music. She encircled his neck with her arms, pressing against him, delighting in the feel of his strong muscles against her. She could spend every night like this. Knowing the trip would wind down soon, however, she savored the moments.

She wished she could spend every night with Declan.

They stayed until after midnight then walked to the suite hand in hand.

"I enjoyed the evening," Declan said as he opened their door.

"Me, too," she said.

"Do you think Jacey's back?" he asked.

"I'll check." Back to the job. Savannah crossed the living room and peeked into Jacey's room. The teenager was sound asleep in her bed, her clothes pooled on the floor. Typical teenager, Savannah thought with amusement as she closed the door.

"In bed and asleep," she reported. "Which is

where I'm heading—bed and sleep. Thanks for a wonderful evening," she said, moving to her door. She was in her room in no time. So no awkward will-he-kiss-me-good-night-or-not moment to deal with. No giving herself away by throwing herself into his arms and clinging like a vine.

She regretted the move as soon as the door closed behind her. Taking a breath, she opened it to say she would rejoin him if he wanted, but he was already moving to his room. She closed the door quietly and leaned against it. She was so dumb sometimes.

Or wise. It depended upon how she looked at things.

Over the next two days, Declan, Savannah and Jacey were treated as special guests at the resort. They followed one of the trails for a day of hiking. They enjoyed the pools, especially the one overlooking the valley, with the waterfall they could swim beneath. Nights Jacey spent with the other teenagers and Savannah and Declan spent as if they were a courting couple—dancing, spending time together walking around the grounds to enjoy the evening coolness. They shared time in the hot tub with another couple.

Thursday dawned overcast with the threat of rain. Declan spent most of the morning on the phone with his office. Jacey was going on a trail ride, if the rain held off. The resort had arranged it for the teenagers who were interested.

"You could go to the day-care center and watch the little kids," Jacey said to Savannah as she prepared to leave.

"Do I look like I need something to do?" Savannah asked, amused Jacey would volunteer her.

"What will you do if I'm gone all day?"

"I might have another day at the spa," Savannah said. It wasn't often she got the luxury. She'd pay for it herself, of course, but it might be fun. She wasn't needed to watch Jacey—between her daytime activities with other teens and her evenings spent telling her father all she'd done, Savannah felt superfluous.

Every night Jacey had other plans leaving Savannah and Declan together. She knew she was falling again for Declan in a big way. And that would give her nothing but heartache. She wished she'd stop trying to guess the future. He was attentive. But he had been before. Could she ever stop making comparisons?

Savannah was lying on the massage table almost asleep when a woman from the spa knocked on the door.

"Sorry to interrupt," she said, sticking her head in when she opened it. "There's an emergency and Mr. Murdock has asked to have Miss Williams return to their suite as soon as she can."

"What's happened?" Savannah asked, sitting up and wrapping the sheet around her. "What emergency?"

"I'm not sure, but he wants you to hurry."

In less than five minutes Savannah entered the suite in a rush. No one was there. She went to his room, it was empty. Checking hers and Jacey's, which were also empty, she turned and headed downstairs. Reaching the front desk, she told the woman she'd been asked to return to the suite but no one was there.

"They're in the infirmary." She beckoned over one of the bell men. "Show Miss Williams to the infirmary, please."

What had happened? Savannah hurried after

the man, glad he walked quickly, as if knowing it was urgent.

When she entered the area, she immediately heard Declan. Following the sound of his voice, she peeped around a cubicle curtain and saw Jacey crying, her dad leaning over her, hugging her and rocking her gently.

"What happened?" She rushed to the side of the high bed.

"I fell and broke my ankle," Jacey wailed, crying.

"Honey, don't cry so, it'll be all right," Declan said, hugging her again.

"It hurts," she complained.

"They'll have you fixed up in no time."

"But I won't be able to ride the horses anymore."

"Did you fall from the horse?" Savannah asked, standing by the opposite side of the bed from Declan, brushing back the hair from Jacey's forehead.

"No. We got off at a look-out point. We were playing around and then I slipped on some rocks and fell a little way, but my foot landed wrong. Stupid old bones. It wasn't that big a fall."

"Sometimes just the oddest angle will be enough," Savannah said. She looked at Declan. He looked totally distraught.

"She'll be okay," she said softly, reaching over to touch him, to offer what support and comfort she could.

"That doesn't make it any easier to deal with," he said. "This changes everything. As soon as her ankle's set, I'm making arrangements to return home."

# CHAPTER SEVEN

LESS than twenty-four hours later they arrived at Declan's apartment. Jacey was exhausted and unhappy. She'd wanted to stay and spend more time with the new friends she'd made at the resort. Declan, however, had finished his business and saw no reason to remain at the resort when it would be easier to care for her at home.

"Want to go lie down?" he asked his daughter when they reached their flat.

"I guess. I'm so tired." Jacey had been grumpy on the flight, unable to become totally comfortable even in the spacious first-class seats. She had not mastered the crutches yet and was clumsy and awkward. Stubborn to the end, however, she managed to go down the hall to her room.

"I'll settle her," Savannah said, following.

A few minutes later she returned to the living room. "She'll be asleep in no time," she murmured. "If you don't need me anymore, I'll head out."

He turned and looked at her.

"Technically, I guess you could say the job's ended. But if you'd stay a few more days of the assignment, it'll help with the transition. The doctor said she could be switched to a walking cast in another week or two. Until then, she's going to need extra help. The venue's changed, but not the timing. Stay, please. Finish the week at least."

"I can't stay beyond that. I have another assignment starting soon."

"Until then."

"You have a housekeeper and are only a few minutes away when you're at work. She's fourteen, she doesn't need a babysitter at home."

He rubbed the back of his neck and shook his head. "We can't just end this like that."

For a moment Savannah felt a spark of hope. Could she finish the assignment here in Manhattan? Spend a few more days—and evenings?—with Declan? The trip was over, but it didn't have to mean *they* were.

"I could come during the day. I do have to

check my schedule. When my next assignment comes up, I need to take it," she said, already deciding to extend her interaction with Declan as long as she could.

He nodded. "I appreciate your help now."

The way his dark eyes looked into hers, Savannah couldn't help hoping. Was it her own imagination, her own yearning? Or was there something more?

She was far too interested and attracted to the man for her own good. And she feared spending more time in his own home would only strengthen that attraction until she'd be in for another huge heartbreak when she left.

A few kisses, quiet times together, dancing the night away—these did not add up to a confession of undying love.

Still, there was nothing to be done about it now. She'd guard her heart and do the best she could.

"Actually, there won't be a housekeeper for a few days. I gave Mrs. Harris the same time off as I was planning to take. I thought we'd be gone. I can have food brought in. You won't have to cook or anything."

"Oh, I don't mind. I enjoy cooking and rarely

get to since I travel so much. When I'm home, I do all the cooking. Stacey doesn't like it that much so the kitchen is my domain." She was already thinking of some of his favorite meals, the ones they'd made together and shared before.

"I'd love some home cooking. But don't feel obligated. You were hired for a different role."

It came down to that. She'd been hired to spend time with his daughter. Any romantic overtones were only in her imagination. Turning away, she tried to catch her breath against the pain that hit her sharply. Was that his way of saying don't get involved? Don't read more into anything?

"Maybe Jacey likes to cook, too. Once she's on her feet again, maybe she'd want to help."

His expression sobered. "I don't even know that about my own daughter. How could a father not know that?"

"Probably because you never gave her a chance. With her mother cooking at home and Mrs. Harris here, it'd be surprising if she did cook."

"Something more to learn. My hope is now that she changed back to the girl I know, she doesn't revert to the Goth creation because we're home."

"It might help if she had friends over."

"Unless they dress all in black."

He walked over to her and placed his hands on her shoulders. Savannah raised her gaze to his, longing for him to pull her close and kiss her.

"I appreciate your help. I'm still technically on vacation, so I won't go into the office for a couple of days. Between the two of us, maybe we can keep the change going."

She felt butterflies in her stomach. His eyes looked into hers and she felt as if she were beginning to float away. Involuntarily her gaze dropped to his mouth. His lips had kissed her, drawn a response from her that had her feeling giddy. Was she the only one to feel it? Once before she'd been in love with Declan Murdock. She felt the same way again.

He squeezed her shoulder and removed his hands, turning to go into the kitchen. "We can check the supplies and see what we need to get to eat for the next few days," he said.

She took a breath, trying to get her racing heart under control. She couldn't have been so foolish as to fall for him again. Had she learned nothing from the past?

But a voice seemed to whisper—again? Had

she ever fallen out of love with him? She'd been hurt, incredibly hurt. Yet she had understood his actions after years of questioning things. He'd tried to do the honorable thing for his daughter, for the mother of his child.

Truth be told, had he known the extent of her love? They'd said it a few times, but only in passion. She'd never told him how she counted the moments until she saw him again. That a part of her felt missing when he was gone. Of the dreams she'd had of the two of them together against the world.

In the end, it hadn't mattered. She doubted if he would have made a different decision.

Savannah stood rooted to the spot. He still hadn't a clue how deeply she felt about him. She should be grateful, but a small part of her wished he felt the same pull of attraction. Wished that he found it hard to act casually and not give in to desire that rose every time they came near each other.

Playing house. That's what it felt like. Declan leaned against the counter in the kitchen and watched as Savannah and Jacey prepared dinner. They were having hamburgers and salad, but the elaborate concoction they were making was fancier than any hamburger he'd ever eaten. He enjoyed watching them. Quite a change from the beginning of the trip two weeks ago. Gone was the sullen girl determined to stay with her mother.

It was like a family ought to be, he thought. Working together, enjoying each other's company. It didn't take money or exotic locales to make him happy. This is what he'd wanted for Jacey all along, once he'd learned of her existence.

The sad part was that this was all make-believe. His second go-round with Margo had ended in shambles despite all the effort he'd made. He wanted the best for his daughter. His ex-wife wanted the best for herself.

What would life have been like if he'd stayed with Savannah, married her and made a home for Jacey with Savannah? That choice had only briefly been entertained seven years ago. She'd still been in college. He couldn't saddle her with a seven-year-old daughter, limit her own activities and future to take on his daughter.

He hadn't wanted Jacey shuttled back and forth between two homes. Yet that's how it ended up.

Some said love conquered all. Love lasted forever.

He didn't think he'd ever loved Margo. Not the way he should have. Never the way he'd felt about Savannah. But he'd tried to do what he thought was right. He wanted to have a family, do things the way his parents had done. Margo had not changed. It appeared she never would.

"Declan, is one enough?" Savannah asked. The way both of them were looking at him, he suspected it wasn't the first time she'd asked.

"Yes. You're making them huge."

"They'll shrink up a bit when cooking," she said, shaping a patty.

Jacey looked at him. "These'll be the best burgers you ever ate."

"Think so?"

"Definitely." She shaped another patty and soon the burgers were broiling in his oven. Savannah instructed Jacey on the next stage. The teen followed instructions perfectly and beamed with the praise Savannah gave when the task was finished.

Once again Declan wondered what things would have been like if he'd made a different choice. He looked at Savannah and felt the desire rise as it did every time he looked at her. She was beautiful, inside and out. She gave more than she took. She was settled and content with her life.

Which was both good and bad. Settled meant she didn't want to change.

He pushed away from the counter. "I'll be back in a minute," he said, leaving the kitchen. He'd made his choice seven years ago. It hadn't worked out at all like he'd hoped. Now, he was stuck with the fallout of that decision.

It didn't matter that some nights he was so lonely he walked outside just to escape the thoughts that crowded his head. That he felt awkward at his own company's picnics in the summer, odd man out because he didn't have his family with him.

He went to the window and stared out across Central Park. It was a windy day, he could see the trees limbs moving. If Jacey were more mobile, they could go to the park. Or someplace. Staying at home, playing house, seeing how well

Savannah fitted into his life brought too many conflicting emotions to the forefront.

The phone rang and he picked it up, hoping it might be work with an emergency needing his attention.

It was Margo.

"I got a text from Jacey that she broke her ankle. Now you're home. How is she?"

"Healing. She'll get a walking cast in another couple of weeks. Until then she's on crutches."

"How did that happen? Were you too busy with work to pay attention to your own daughter?"

"She was well looked after. She was horse-back-riding with friends. They stopped and got to playing around. She slipped on some rocks," he answered patiently, ignoring the other part of her comment.

"She should come back home."

"She is home, with me. For the summer. I thought you wanted it that way."

"I did, things changed. You'll be away at work more than you'll be home," Margo said.

"You work, how is that different?" Declan asked.

The silence lasted only a moment, then she

said, "I could take a leave if you'd make up the difference in pay. Then I'd be home with her all summer."

"Not going to happen. She's mine for the summer."

"I'm coming to see her," Margo said.,

"Not today. Come tomorrow if you like. We'll be here."

Hanging up, Declan wished he could keep the woman as far away from Jacey as possible. Maybe he should consider asking his daughter now if she'd like to live with him for the next few years. All too soon she'd be off to college and her own future. If she was to be his only child, he should spend more time with her. He'd hoped waiting until later in the summer would give her a sense of how they would live, which would help her make up her mind. Maybe waiting would be a mistake.

"Dad, dinner's ready," Jacey called.

Back to playing house. Savannah would be gone soon and life would return to normal.

The next morning Savannah headed for Declan's early. She planned to make omelets for breakfast and had picked up some cinnamon buns for an extra treat. Normally she didn't like sweets with breakfast, but she had a soft spot for cinnamon buns. She hoped Declan and Jacey did, too.

Riding the elevator, she tried to quell her anticipation of seeing Declan again. Last night had been low-key, and when she'd left for home Jacey had even asked if she'd be back. When she'd heard Savannah would bring breakfast, she'd seemed delighted. "You can teach me how to make omelets. I've always wanted to know."

Declan's daughter was turning out to be a lot of fun. He was right in insisting she stay with him, the change in such a short time was amazing. Savannah even hoped Jacey liked her, as well.

Knocking on the door, she was impatient for it to open. When Jacey opened it, she smiled.

"Good morning."

"Did you bring the eggs?"

Savannah held up one bag.

"Something smells good," Jacey said, looking at the other one.

"Cinnamon rolls."

Savannah held the bag out of reach and headed for the kitchen, telling Jacey what she'd brought.

"I want one," the teen said, following on her crutches.

"After the omelet. You'll love my omelets, they are light and full of goodies."

"Like what?" Jacey lumbered along on her crutches.

Savannah smiled at Declan when she entered the kitchen. He was standing by the coffeemaker, waiting for the pot to fill. "Good morning to you." Seeing him had her catching her breath again. He looked so inviting. If Jacey weren't around, would he have kissed her? His gaze flicked to her mouth and she felt it almost like a caress.

If Jacey wasn't around, however, there'd be no need for Savannah to be there.

"I heard about the food. Maybe we should eat the buns while you're cooking the omelets," he suggested, eyeing the white paper bag.

"Nice try. I want you both to appreciate my cooking expertise."

Jacey stood by the door. "I'm making a note-book for cooking. I'll be right back. Don't start without me."

She turned and thumped down the hall toward her bedroom.

Declan grinned and stepped forward, sweeping Savannah into his arms, bending her back theatrically and giving her a big kiss. She clung—to avoid falling she assured herself. But for an instant, all thought fled and only the feelings his kiss engendered roiled through her. All too soon he brought her back upright and released her.

"Wow," Savannah said, staring at him in surprise.

"I didn't get a good-night kiss last night," he said, turning and taking cups from the cupboard.

Jacey could be heard returning.

Savannah turned and began blindly searching for a bowl, her mind roiling. The kiss had been over too soon. Her heart pounded. She desperately hoped he couldn't tell. It was one thing to play along, something else again to hide her true feelings.

Breakfast was accompanied by laughter and jokes and plans for the rest of the summer. Savannah listened and joined in where she thought appropriate. She felt a hint of sadness that she wouldn't be participating in all the activities Declan planned, like trips to the beach when the ankle was healed, a weekend in the Adirondacks.

She remembered one weekend they'd spent there. Would she ever remember the past without the weight of the end of their relationship?

While she was washing the dishes, Declan and Jacey still sat at the table, Jacey looked over at her. "Do you know where you'll be next?"

"I'm leaving next week for a cruise of the Norwegian fjords," she said. She'd checked in with Stephanie at the office and been given her next assignment. The days were counting down.

"For how long?" Declan asked.

"Two weeks."

"You'll be gone for two weeks?" Jacey repeated. "I thought you'd be around and go with us to the movies or a play or something."

"Your father hired me for the trip to California, not the entire summer. This is my busiest time."

Savannah felt oddly bereft thinking of leaving at the end of the week and not seeing Declan or Jacey again. But that was the way Vacation Nannies worked. She had a new assignment and would have another after that.

Jacey looked perplexed. She looked at her dad. "Can't you hire her for the rest of the summer?"

He drew his coffee closer and looked at his

daughter. "Savannah has a job to do. You and I don't need her. We'll manage fine on our own. Establish routines that suit us."

"But you could pay her to stay with me," Jacey said.

"I could. But she has other obligations. She's already agreed to go with the other family to Norway. She can't go back on her word."

Jacey studied her father for a moment. Declan nodded slowly, hoping Jacey would understand. He was having a hard time himself, but dared not show it.

Jacey was quiet for a long moment, then said, "Like Mom does?"

He didn't know how to answer that. The truth was hard to take. "It's different with your mother. She and I had a relationship. We were married. But we changed. The marriage didn't last. I'm sorry that it didn't. It wasn't your fault."

"It was Mom's fault," Jacey said slowly. "I think she just wants your money."

"I'm not obligated to support her once the legal tie was severed," Declan said slowly.

"That doesn't mean your dad doesn't want to help you," Savannah said when Jacey looked as if she were contemplating what Declan had said. "He sends money for you. If you lived with him instead of your mother, he'd still spend money on you. You're his daughter—he'll support you until you're grown."

"And then I have to stand on my own two feet?" Jacey asked, looking at Savannah and then her father.

He nodded. "For the most part."

"Even though you have oodles of money?"

"It's your dad who has oodles of money, not you," Savannah said softly.

"That's not fair," Jacey said.

"How is it not fair? If you earned a lot of money, wouldn't you want the right to choose how you spent it? Would you want to feel obligated to give it to someone else—even a close family member?" Savannah asked.

The teen considered the situation for a few moments, then reluctantly shrugged. "I guess I'd want to have the final say in how my money was spent. But I'd want my family to be happy, too."

"Money doesn't buy happiness," Declan said, with a look at Savannah.

"It buys a lot of stuff," Jacey retorted.

"More to clean, store, worry about breaking or being taken," Savannah suggested, wiping the last of the counter and rinsing the cloth.

"I like a lot of things," Jacey said.

"All the more reason to do well in school, go to college and get a good-paying job," Declan said.

Jacey rolled her eyes and shook her head. "You're always saying that."

Declan laughed. "Is it sinking in?"

Jacey wrinkled her nose and shrugged. "I guess."

There was a knock on the door.

"Who even knows we're home?" he asked, rising.

Jacey watched him walk to the door. "My mom knows," she said slowly as her father left the kitchen.

Savannah heard the voices and suspected Jacey was right, Margo had arrived.

Jacey got up and clumped to the living room. Savannah followed.

Margo Murdock was tall and thin with brown hair and a frown on her face. She had been talking with Declan, but now looked at her daughter, who was struggling to get to her mother on her crutches.

"Oh, my poor baby. Look at you. Does it hurt?" She walked swiftly across the room and gave Jacey a hug, almost knocking her over as one of the crutches was dislodged.

"Let her get to the sofa first, Margo," Declan said, moving to intercept.

"I'm going to be okay, Mom. My ankle throbs a little, but it's not too bad." She lumbered to the sofa and then sank down, placing the crutches on the floor.

Margo followed and sat beside her. She brushed back her daughter's hair. "I see you've changed your hair again."

"Yeah. I went to a spa and a complete make-over was included. It was really cool. They had massages, and did my toenails." Jacey wiggled her toes and looked hopefully at her mother, but Margo turned away and glared at Declan.

"She needs to come home. You need to provide a nurse so she'll be taken care of."

"Mom, I'm okay."

"I thought you wanted her to spend the summer with me. What happened to your plans that made it impossible for Jacey to stay home with you?" Declan asked.

Savannah stood by the table, watching the scenario unfold. She'd have been a lot more frustrated than Declan appeared to be. From all Jacey had said since she'd met her, Savannah felt Margo would propose anything if she thought she'd get more money.

How had Declan fallen for her? Granted she was a beautiful woman, but some of that was due to cosmetics and clothes. Too bad her personality didn't match.

*Meow,* she thought. For a moment she considered leaving. But something kept her in place. Jacey was scowling. Margo looked peeved and Declan had lost that easygoing air and now looked decidedly angry.

"Coffee anyone? I can make some," she said, to break the tension.

"I'll take a cup," Declan said.

"I'd like a cup, as well. You remember how I like it, Declan," Margo said, still sitting beside her daughter.

"Black?" he asked.

She pouted for a second and shook her head. "Cream and just a small teaspoon of sugar."

Declan reached Savannah and put his arm across her shoulders, urging her into the kitchen. "The more I'm around that woman, the more I want to pull my hair out. She drives me up the wall," he said, dropping his arm when they were out of view.

Savannah pulled down three mugs and put them on the counter, then waited for the coffee to drip into the pot.

"You hide that so well," she murmured.

He gave a short laugh. "I made a mistake even talking to her last night. I wish she hadn't come today. I can't believe her nerve, wanting me to pay her to watch our daughter if she took a leave of absence from work. She just wants a summer off."

Savannah didn't know how to respond. She was totally unimpressed with Margo Murdock. How had Declan ever thought the two of them were suited?

Declan leaned against the counter, watching Savannah prepare the coffee mugs. "Actually I think Jacey *wants* to stay here this summer."

"Good for her. I think the two of you have re-captured some of the relationship you had be-fore," Savannah said, taking the full pot and pouring coffee into three mugs.

He reached over and cupped Savannah's chin, turning her face toward him. "I have you to thank for the change."

The touch of his fingers tingled through her as she watched him. His frustration rolled off him. Then he seemed to really see her and his touch softened. His thumb caressed her jaw gently.

"I know it's above and beyond what you usu-ally get when hired. But I needed your help."

"I owe you for all the information you so freely shared in class. Vacation Nannies wouldn't be the success we are if you hadn't."

For a second Savannah thought she glimpsed disappointment.

He dropped his hand and nodded. "Gratitude? Was that—never mind. Not that I need it. I was paid for my lectures."

She picked up his cup and the one prepared for Margo and handed them both to him.

"Ready for round two?"

She nodded. "Wait a minute."

Both his hands were full, but she didn't pick up her own cup. Instead, she reached up to cradle his face in her palms and pulled his head down to kiss him on the mouth. She could feel his startled surprise. A moment later she pulled back, studying him for a moment.

"For luck," she said.

"Next time give a bit of warning. I almost dropped the cups."

*If there ever will be a next time,* she thought sadly.

Margo looked suspiciously at them both when they returned. Taking her cup, she glared at Savannah.

"This is a family matter," she said.

"Savannah stays," Declan said.

Margo changed her gaze. "Honestly, Declan," she said, ignoring Savannah, "how could you put Jacey at risk like that? She could have been more seriously injured."

"Chill, Mom, it was my own fault. And it wasn't as if I fell off the horse. I was already on the ground, scrambling around some rocks."

Margo glanced at her daughter then back at Declan. "She needs someone with her."

He shrugged. "I'll take more time off. Mrs. Harris will be back next week. Jacey will get a walking cast soon and be good to go—right, sweetheart?"

"Yep," Jacey said, grinning at her father.

Margo fumed.

Jacey looked at her. "Maybe Mom could see me on a weekend," she suggested.

"I don't think that's a good idea," Declan said.

"I don't see why you two can't get married again and we'd all live together!"

Savannah saw the work of the past two weeks unraveling with the presence of Jacey's mother. She looked at Declan and her heart went out to him. He'd tried too hard to let this happen now. Desperate for something that would help, she racked her brains. Then an idea hit.

"I know someone who lives in the Hamptons," she said. Looking directly at Margo, she continued, "How about if I ask if you can use their guest cottage for a week or two this summer? You'd have to work around any guests they've already invited, but I bet there would be a couple of weeks still available. Free, of course."

Margo narrowed her eyes. "Why would you do such a thing?"

"To get you to leave," she said frankly.

Declan swung his gaze to Savannah in astonishment. Jacey looked at her mother and back at Savannah.

"I can get two weeks off in August," Margo said slowly. "That would give me time to get some new clothes, too."

"Mom, what about me?" Jacey asked.

"Honey, you're going to be incapacitated for weeks with that cast, most of your summer actually. You don't want to get a tan line from mid-calf up. We'll talk on the phone. It's obvious your father doesn't want me around."

Jacey frowned. "But I do."

"Honey, this is your time with your father. Once fall gets here, we'll be like we were."

Jacey didn't looked convinced.

Declan wanted to hug Savannah right then and there. Was this going to work? Would Margo just up and leave now that she had something she wanted? And how did Savannah know anyone in the Hamptons? He wouldn't have thought Vacation Nannies moved in those circles.

Unless—it had to be a former client. Someone she'd worked for before. Did she have such a good relationship that they'd do her such a huge favor? He felt a ping of jealousy. He wished he knew more about her life, more about her friends.

Margo glanced at her watch. "Oh, dear, I need to get going. I'm only going in a bit late, not taking the day off." When she rose, she looked at Savannah. "Jacey has my phone number. Call and let me know so I can get the time off."

Savannah nodded.

Once Declan shut the door behind Margo he turned back to the room. "A stroke of genius," he said. "Do you really have friends there who might let her use their guest cottage for two weeks?"

She nodded. "The Hendersons. I'll call this morning."

"Are they old?" Jacey asked.

Savannah looked at her in surprise. "What does that matter?"

"'Cause I think Mom only wants to go there so she can meet a rich husband. She's said so the last two times she's gone. But those have only been weekend parties and no available men were there."

"The Hendersons are probably a few years older than your mother. I watched their kids a couple of times. Your mother would not be part of their social network, just have use of the cottage. But she could go into town, find friends there."

Declan couldn't believe Margo would be so forthright with their daughter about her desire to marry money. He didn't want to marry again without love and the happy union his parents had had. He didn't want Jacey to think of marriage as a way to get money or an extravagant lifestyle.

He looked at Savannah, calmly sitting sipping her coffee. He wished he could emulate her serenity. Seeing Margo always hit a hot button. It reminded him of his loss seven years ago. Of a foolish decision that had never gone the way he'd hoped, but that had ended the best thing in his life.

"I'm going to my room," Jacey said, struggling to get off the sofa.

When she'd left, he turned to Savannah. "Now what?"

"Up to you."

"I want to spend time with her. I'll have to go into work from time to time, a couple of days a week, but this is my summer to get to know my daughter in all her facets."

"Jacey's lucky to have you for a dad," she said.

"Not so lucky in her mother," he replied.

Savannah shrugged. "Margo has different values. She wants to get ahead, like everyone else."

"She wants to get ahead the easy way, the best way for Margo. I want my daughter to be caring and content, not constantly unhappy because of the way her life is going."

"So tell her. Spend time sharing your values and expectations. Let her know what you want for her life, and then support her the best you can."

"How did you get so smart about teenagers?"

She laughed. "Not so smart, just some common sense. I was a teenager once."

"And not too long ago."

"Long enough to look back and see things a bit more objectively. Anyway, if you don't need me any longer, I'll take off."

"I do need you. Stay. Don't let me face Jacey alone yet."

"You're joking, right?"

"Maybe a little. But things do go more smoothly when you're around."

It was on the tip of Savannah's tongue to say things could go more smoothly always if he'd keep her around. She'd stay, she'd make memories, and when she left she wouldn't look back.

# CHAPTER EIGHT

SAVANNAH called the office to check in and to get the phone number for the Hendersons. She then called them and chatted for a few moments before asking her favor. They discussed the situation for a little while, Savannah implying Margo was a friend, though she knew the two of them never would be. Still, for the sake of getting her away from Declan and Jacey for the summer, she'd say almost anything.

"Great, thanks a bunch. I appreciate this more than you'll know," she said when they'd agreed to two weeks in August. "May I talk to Patty now?" The little girl was a special favorite of hers. She'd watched her several times in the past three years and was scheduled again at Thanksgiving when the entire family was flying to Hawaii.

She spoke with Patty for almost ten minutes, then said goodbye.

"You really like her, don't you?' Declan asked.

He'd been lounging on the sofa during her call, watching Savannah's animation as she talked to both the parents and the child, amazed she would do such a favor for his ex-wife.

"Patty is a little doll. She had the sweetest disposition I've ever come across. I keep in touch with some of my kids."

"Come sit by me and tell me more," he said.

She rose and sat beside him on the sofa. He was glad she hadn't argued.

But as he took her hand and laced their fingers, resting them on his thigh, he remembered back to when they'd sit after dinner and talk. As she talked about some of her kids he remembered how much he'd liked listening to her. She was entertaining, yet her own values shone through. She was the kind of person he wanted his daughter to grow up to be. Caring, kind, taking delight in mundane things, yet charting her future with goals and working to achieve everything on her terms.

He watched her as smiles lit her face. She genuinely liked the children she watched. And obviously she loved the travel. It tugged at his heart.

He'd missed her over the years. Was there any chance—

Jacey came out of her room a short time later, while both of them were laughing at a story Savannah had told.

His daughter sat on a chair and looked at them, noting the held hands. Her eyes widened and Declan quickly released Savannah's hand.

"What's funny?" she asked.

"Savannah has a way of telling a story that has me laughing," Declan said. "Tell her about Maisie May."

Savannah smiled. "You want to hear it again?"

"Why not? I bet it's just as funny the second time."

So Savannah related the experience she'd had with a Cajun woman who was sure she could cast a spell to find her a husband. She embellished it a bit more this time around and before long Jacey was laughing.

"How did you meet her?" she asked at the end of the story.

Savannah explained how she'd had a few days extra in New Orleans and had gone exploring. That led to more questions from Jacey about her job.

After she finished there was a moment of quiet. Jacey looked at her dad again.

"You're never going to marry Mom again, are you?"

He shook his head.

"Are you and Savannah going to get married?"

Declan went on alert, his gaze seeking Savannah's.

"No," Savannah said, rising.

"But if Dad asked you, why wouldn't you say yes, then if you two got married, I could live here, couldn't I?"

Declan felt his heart catch. "You could live here with me whether or not I ever marry again," he said, trying not to give away how much it meant to him.

"I think I'm in Mom's way," she said slowly.

"Oh, honey, I'm sure that's not true. I'd love for you to come live with me if you want to. You already have your room, know the neighborhood. It'd mean changing schools, but you could handle that easily enough."

Jacey smiled. "Well, I'll think about it."

"You do that, honey. I'd love to have you spend your high school years here. Before you know it, you'll be grown and out the door and on your own," Declan said.

Jacey looked thoughtful as she nodded again. "I'll think about it. I don't have to decide now, do I?"

"No, we have all summer to decide. But we do need to let your mom know when you're ready," Declan said.

Savannah wondered how Margo would take the news. Maybe Jacey was cramping her style, but she also was the reason Margo got a generous child support check each month. How would she feel about that vanishing?

"So, what shall we do today?" Jacey asked. "How about a movie? That way I can sit most of the time."

They agreed on a movie and once lunch was over, they headed out to the nearest theater. It wasn't crowded, even though school was out. Sitting near the center, Declan sat between the two of them, and once the theater went dark, he reached for Savannah's hand.

She looked at him but only saw him studying the screen as the previews played.

She would be hard-pressed to concentrate on the movie when her entire focus was on the sensations cascading through her at his touch. She sat in the dark, eyes on the big screen, her thoughts tumbled and confused. The more she was around him, the more she wanted to be with him. Yet he never spoke of the past or the future.

When the lights came on at the end, she blinked and pulled her hand away. Following Jacey and Declan out of the row, she made up her mind to go home now, not to spend another minute with the man. She had to gain some distance and per-spective. The only change she'd seen this sum-mer was that her love had been brought to the forefront. It had been hidden and now she had to face it again.

Letting Jacey get ahead of them a little bit as they exited the theater, she said softly, "I'm going home. If you need me tomorrow I'll come over. But I think the two of you get along better than ever now. You don't need me any longer." It was hard to say the words.

"Stay for dinner."

"No. You need time alone with Jacey and I need some time alone myself."

His eyes looked into hers. "Why?"

"Why what?" She felt her senses scatter.

"Why do you need time alone?"

"I just do." She looked away, seeing Jacey near the doors to the outside, watching them.

"We're limited in what we can do while she's in that cast. Another summer we could go to the beach, do some museums, other things, but not right now. You have ideas on how to entertain children. I need you. You said until the end of the week. Come on with us, Savannah."

*I need you.* How she wished it was for more than entertaining his daughter.

"Okay, I'll come back for a little while. We could play board games. Do you have any?"

"No."

"Then we need to swing by a toy store on the way back to your place."

Jacey balked initially at the suggestion of playing games, declaring it was too childish. But once they were back at Declan's apartment, she grew more enthusiastic. And once she beat her father at Yahtzee, she wanted to play even more.

Declan called for dinner from a nearby Chinese

restaurant. Once dinner was finished, he said he'd take Savannah home.

"I can grab a cab," she said, putting away the games.

"I'll take you. You'll be okay here for a short while, right?" he asked his daughter.

"Sure. I'll watch television until you get back. Then I want a rematch on checkers." That had been the game Declan beat her on every time.

"Better study up on strategy, then," he teased.

She laughed. Coming over to Savannah, she balanced on her crutches and gave her a hug. "Thanks for today, it was fun."

"I had fun, too." Savannah was touched at the teen's show of affection. What a difference in such a short time.

Declan flagged down a cab and they settled in the back seat.

"I can't believe she might want to come live with me," he said as the cab pulled out into traffic.

"I think it's great. You'll be a better influence on her than her mother," Savannah said.

"There might be a problem getting Margo to agree to changing the custody agreement."

"Probably not as much as you think. You should ask your attorney," Savannah said.

"I will. Thanks for today. It's the most fun I've had in ages. And all because of you."

"Now you have some ideas of how to entertain her until she's more mobile. I hope you both have the best of summers."

"That sounds like goodbye."

"It is. Declan, you hired me for the trip to California. That's been cut short. The longer we play at this, the harder it's going to be at the end."

He was silent for a moment, staring out the side window. Then he turned and looked at her. "What if we don't stop seeing each other?"

"What do you mean?" For a moment, hope blossomed. Then her spirits fell. "I'm booked most of the summer. I won't be around."

"Can't someone else take your assignments? I can pay for the entire summer."

Pay for her time? She was hoping for a renewed relationship and he was talking about hiring her to spend time with his daughter.

She shook her head. "Some of these families are repeat clients and asked especially for me. I'm not going to send someone else in my place."

They arrived at her apartment building.

"Wait, please," Declan told the cabdriver. "I'm just escorting her to her apartment." He slipped the man a twenty-dollar bill and opened the car door.

The ride in the elevator was silent. Savannah wished things could end differently, but she didn't see how anything had changed.

Declan walked beside her to her door, trying to find a compelling reason she should stay.

"How about dinner tomorrow night, just you and me?" he said as she took her keys from her purse.

She looked at him. "Dinner?"

"That's right, the evening meal. Dress up, we'll go some place nice."

He could tell she didn't think it was a good idea. "Consider it a bonus for the excellent job you did for me." *And give me the opportunity to change your mind about leaving,* he added silently.

"Okay then. Will Jacey be all right?"

"I'll make sure. Maybe she could invite a friend over to keep her company. I'll pick you up at seven."

Savannah hesitated, then nodded. "Okay. Good night."

She had the door open. But he wasn't going to let her go so easily. He pulled her gently into his arms and kissed her, letting her know the only way he knew how that she was someone special. He didn't understand why he was so anxious to stay involved, but he wasn't letting her go so soon. He wanted more time with Savannah.

When she responded, he deepened the kiss. Her sweet curves met his harder muscles in all the right places. He could have held her all night. Memories crowded, the present vanished and it was as if he was reluctantly parting from her for the night seven years ago. She had a class early in the morning or he had a new product to consider. They'd meet again tomorrow night.

For a moment he forgot what had happened. Reality crashed down when she pushed him slightly. He let her go, staring down into her big blue eyes. He saw the hurt, the uncertainty and the distrust. All the emotions he'd caused.

He wanted to rail at fate for the way things had ended. The way he'd thought to make things right. How could doing wrong to this lovely woman ever have seemed right?

"Good night, Declan."

He stood in front of her closed door for another minute. She'd entered her apartment too quickly. And for a moment, he'd felt her farewell was final. At least he had tomorrow evening to get her to change her mind. Slowly he returned to the cab.

"Take a longer route home, I have some thinking to do," he instructed the cabby.

"You got it, mister. That's a first, asking for a longer way," the man replied, shaking his head in amazement.

When Declan returned home, Jacey was snuggled down on the sofa, a light afghan over her. The show on the TV was a comedy. She looked up when he came in. "I've been thinking," she said, sitting up and switching off the TV with the remote. "I would like to come here to live."

"I'd do almost anything to have you live with me a few years. You're sure?"

"Yes. I think Mom'll like being on her own. She complains sometimes that I take a lot of work. It won't be too much work for you, will it?"

"Never." He felt love sweep through him for this sweet child of his.

"What are you going to do when I'm gone off to college? You'll be all alone."

Did every woman no matter what the age think being alone was worse than being in a marriage just for the sake of companionship?

"I'll manage. I've been alone these past few years."

"But I used to come to visit on weekends and the summer."

"You won't drop in from time to time once you're off to college?" he asked.

"Sure, sometimes. But I'll be busy at school and with friends. Dad, you should think about marrying Savannah. She's nice."

He sat up and looked at her seriously. "Let's discuss your moving here—what ramifications we can expect and when to tell your mother." He didn't even want to think about marrying Savannah. If he'd only done so when he'd had the chance. How different would all their lives be now?

When Declan picked up Savannah at seven the next evening he had a good game strategy in mind. Jacey was going to live with him. He was very appreciative of that. Next week he'd return to the office and work a minimum schedule, making up any lost time when at home in the evenings. The rest of the day he and Jacey could spend together.

Knocking on the door, he thought he should have asked Savannah out before, after he'd divorced Margo. He hadn't because he'd thought she'd moved on. He hadn't been able to bear the thought of finding a new man in her life.

Savannah opened the door looking as lovely as he'd ever seen her. The blue dress she wore reflected her own eyes. Her smile rocked him to his toes. He'd missed her over the years.

"You're on time and I'm ready. Just let me get my purse." She picked up a small clutch and put her keys inside.

He stepped in, crowding her a bit and leaned for a quick brush of his lips against hers. She reminded him of happiness, love, family and youth.

She looked up in surprise.

He had kept the cab waiting and soon they were off to the Bradbury, one of the latest trendy restaurants. Situated on the top of one of the high-rise hotels on Broadway, it was a short cab ride. They rode an outside glass elevator which gave them a beautiful view of Times Square and surrounding buildings. Soon they reached the top floor and stepped right into the restaurant.

Savannah had heard about this place, but had never eaten here before. She was surprised to see that beyond the bar there was a dance floor. The seating for the restaurant was to their right. Declan had obviously made reservations. After escorting them to one of the tables beside the floor-to-ceiling windows, the maître d' pulled out a chair for Savannah.

"Wow, good thing I'm not afraid of heights," she said a moment later when Declan sat opposite her. "This view is amazing. And I feel like I'm a bird perched somewhere, able to see for miles."

"Glad you like it. I've only been once before. The food's good, too."

Declan waited until they'd ordered then told her about his day with his daughter.

Savannah listened and smiled a time or two. He couldn't help feel that the day would have been even more special had she been with them.

Then he told her of their discussion on Jacey's

moving in. "I want expectations to be clear on both ends. And to make sure she's really going through with it. I'm worried about Margo's reaction. She's not going to be happy and I don't want her pressuring Jacey."

"Jacey will have to be very sure of her decision to stand up to her mother. But I think it'll be the best thing for both of them in the long run," Savannah said.

Savannah looked out the window. He followed her gaze and studied the view for a few minutes. It was spectacular. The sky would turn red with the sunset soon and once darkness fell the lights of the city would glimmer like stars.

"I have news," Savannah said. "My sister's engaged! To the man who hired her to watch his children on the trip to Spain. She got the assignment because she speaks the language. Now she'll spend some of her time there and some here in New York."

"What's she going to do about Vacation Nannies?" Declan asked.

"We haven't discussed that in depth yet. She's asked Stephanie to stop booking her until she gets back and we discuss things. I see big changes ahead. I hope we can get another Spanish-speaking nanny, we have a call for one several times a year."

"You don't speak it?" he asked.

"No, English only. I think we should have planned for something like this, but both of us were so full of starting our business and getting ahead, we never planned for one of us bailing out."

"Is that how it feels, as though she's bailing out?"

Savannah tilted her head in thought. Declan loved that look.

"Not really. She'll still be involved. Mostly I'm happy for her. She sounded so happy on the phone. And I spoke with her fiancé and the two boys. They arrived in New York, and then two weeks later turned around and flew back to Spain to celebrate with his family."

"Do you think she'll keep working?"

"Not if traveling is needed. I think she plans to stay home with Luis's boys—at least initially."

"Does that happen often—a nanny leaves for marriage?"

"Usually that's the only way our nannies leave.

We have a great business and properly trained nannies love the idea of all the travel."

Declan changed the subject of conversation to veer away from marriages. If things had gone differently seven years ago, he and Savannah might have married. Had children by now.

The thought hit him in the gut. He could have had a home full of children by now. Funny he had no doubt that he and Savannah would have made their marriage work. Would she ever consider marrying him after all that had happened?

When they finished eating, he suggested they stay longer and enjoy the music and dancing. He felt a wave of satisfaction when she agreed. He couldn't wait to hold her in his arms while they danced.

The rest of the evening went perfectly. They danced, enjoyed a nightcap, danced again. When it was finally late enough that he knew they had to leave he requested one more dance.

"I've enjoyed the evening," he said softly. His chin rested against her forehead. He could breathe in her sweet light scent. He'd forever associate it with Savannah and dancing the night away.

"I have, too."

"Come by the house tomorrow. We'll play games, plan the trip to the beach."

"You and Jacey need to do that without me," she said.

"Come anyway," he urged.

She was silent for so long he thought she'd refuse. Finally, she said, "Okay, but for the last time. I'm leaving for two weeks soon and have chores to do around the apartment."

For a moment he wanted to argue. But there was no denying that next week Savannah would be off to another assignment. Off to another country and another family. He didn't like the thought.

The drive back to the apartment took only moments. He felt as if he'd left his best friend behind. Tomorrow he'd ask her out again. Spend as much time as he could with her before she took off on the next assignment. He didn't examine closely why or consider what he'd do if she said no.

# CHAPTER NINE

SAVANNAH took the subway to Declan's neighborhood the next morning and walked the rest of the way. It was one of those perfect New York days. The sky was clear, a light breeze blew. The temperature hadn't risen to an uncomfortable level. She loved New York on days like this. If Jacey hadn't had her broken ankle, they could have walked to the river and enjoyed watching the boats. Or was that too childish for a teenager? She almost laughed aloud. She bet the thought of other teens around would have Jacey jumping at the chance.

She greeted the doorman and was escorted right to the elevator. Rising swiftly to Declan's floor, her anticipation rose as she walked down the hall to his flat.

Knocking on the door, she smiled. She couldn't wait to see him.

Declan opened the door a moment later, a frown

on his face. "We have a problem," he said, opening the door wider and motioning her in.

Jacey sat on the sofa, crying, her crutches leaning against the arm.

"What happened?" Savannah asked, glancing between Jacey and Declan.

"Margo was in a hit-and-run accident last night. She was in a crosswalk and someone knocked her several feet. She's in a coma at the hospital. We were waiting until you got here to go."

"She could be dying," Jacey said, rubbing her face with a soggy handkerchief. "We had to wait until you got here because you didn't answer your phone."

Savannah frowned, remembering she'd left it in the charger when she headed for the bakery this morning. "I'm sorry. You should have gone. You could have left a note."

"I said that to Dad, but he insisted we wait for you."

"They aren't going to let us in to see her anyway, Jacey," Declan said gently. He looked at Savannah. "She's hurt pretty badly. I still need to find out how much."

"What if she dies?" Jacey asked, scared.

"I'm hoping she won't die," he said. "Don't think the worst until we know more facts."

"What can I do?" Savannah asked.

He hesitated a moment, then said, "Can you come with us? I know you probably don't want to, but I could use the support."

Savannah nodded. "I brought cinnamon rolls again. Have you two eaten?"

"I don't want to eat. I want to see Mom," Jacey said, struggling to her feet. "Dad, you said we could leave as soon as Savannah got here."

"I did and we can. Bring the rolls, we'll eat them on the way."

"I'm not hungry," Jacey said. "I hope Mom's going to be okay. You'll help, right, Dad?"

"As much as I can," Declan said.

For a moment Savannah was taken back seven years. This reminded her of what had happened then. Margo needed Declan; he left Savannah to go to her.

Granted, this was a bit different. Margo needed both Declan and Jacey. But was this a pattern that would always be repeated? Declan going to Margo?

"Here," Savannah thrust the white bag into

Declan's hands. "I can't go after all. Sorry." She had decided two days ago to make the break. This was the perfect chance. All her insecurities and uncertainties rose.

Nothing had changed, much as she had wished for it. Seven years ago Margo had arrived back in New York with a child Declan had not known they had. She'd beckoned and he'd gone to her. Now she was injured and needed help. He was going again.

It didn't matter to her that anyone would go to help someone with a tie to the past as Margo had to Declan. It mattered only that Declan was going.

She was not going to be left behind this time.

If she really had a spot in Declan's life, she'd jump in to help as much as she could. But despite a few kisses, nothing had changed. He had never given a hint he wanted anything beyond her services as nanny to his daughter. Her assignment had really finished when they returned to New York. She should have stood firm at leaving then. She might have wondered, but nothing like this would have happened.

"Where are you going?" Declan asked. "I need you."

Savannah shook her head. "You have your family. It's not mine." Foolishly she'd let her love blossom, but she'd known all along heartbreak would follow.

He reached out and took her shoulders gently, turning her so she faced him.

"There's something between us, you know it, I know it."

She gazed into his dear dark eyes. She hoped she never forgot this moment. She could almost imagine he was asking her to stay forever, to make a life with him. To help with Jacey and moving on and getting married and having children.

The reality, however was that he wanted her help with Margo. He'd left her once before for the woman—the woman and child. They were still in the picture.

Could a person feel her heart break? Surely it was just fantasy, yet the pain gripping her chest belied that. She thought it at least cracked.

She wanted to tell him she loved him, see if he'd be willing to open his mind to the possibility of a future together. But nothing he'd said or done gave her hope, it was her own dreamy fantasy.

"I have to go," she said, her voice cracking a bit. Blinking back tears, she reached up to kiss him. He pulled her into his arms, holding her tightly against him, pouring out the attraction and desire that had shimmered between them into that kiss.

Both were breathing hard when Savannah pushed herself free. She tried a smile, but tears welled. Turning swiftly, she went to the door.

"Wait, Savannah," he called.

She shook her head and let herself out of the apartment. Not wanting to wait for the elevator, she slipped out into the stairs, the door closing as she heard him call again. Was he coming after her? Wanting to change the parameters of their agreement? Wanting to say he loved her?

Walking swiftly down the stairs, she listened for any sounds from above. All was silent.

It took her several minutes to go down all the floors. When she pushed open the outside door into the sunshine, she stopped a moment to draw a breath.

The day was still beautiful. The sun shone.

The light breeze kept the temperatures moderate. How could the world look so bright and happy when her life had become dark and dismal?

# CHAPTER TEN

DECLAN stood in the doorway staring down the empty hall. She had gone. Slowly he closed the door. Why had the accident happened? Was fate constantly going to intervene just when he thought he was getting his life the way he wanted it?

Instead of a day together, a day in which he might suggest future outings, he had a heart-sick, scared teenager and an empty spot where Savannah had been moments before.

He rubbed his face with his hands. Maybe she'd come back when she'd had a chance to consider.

Consider what? For a long moment he stared at the hall. Something about this reminded him of his leaving last time.

Margo. Was he to have her in his life forever?

"Dad, can we go?" Jacey came over to him, her worried expression touching his heart. Her mother had been injured. Right now he needed to take care of his daughter. He'd go after Savannah later.

Their original assignment was over. She'd delivered all he'd expected and more. He had nothing more to hold her with. She would be leaving next week on another assignment. For a bright businessman who had built a major company, he had acted like a dumb kid in this.

"Yes, Jacey, we'll go now."

"Why did Savannah kiss you?"

He shrugged. He wasn't going to try to explain why. He could still see the tears in her eyes. "For comfort, I expect."

Savannah went back the her apartment. She was totally unhappy. After a day of feeling sorry for herself, however, the next morning she decided she wasn't giving in to it.

She called her sister. She wanted to hear Stacey's voice and to listen to her happiness with her plans. She exclaimed at all the right places, wishing she had something equally exciting to tell her.

She didn't say a word about her personal situation. If she'd begun, she didn't think she could stop. Her sister would either tell her she was crazy or offer some insight that would help her deal with the situation. But it would dim some of Stacey's happiness and Savannah wouldn't have that for anything.

Once they finished talking, Savannah couldn't sit still. She had a new job in a couple of days. If nothing else, she'd go shopping. She longed for the hustle and bustle of stores, of being anonymous in a crowd. Of something to take her mind off Declan.

She found two outfits that would be suitable for the cruise of the fjords of Norway. She also saw a pretty sundress that would look good on Jacey. Holding it up, she studied it for a moment. On impulse, she added it to the clothes she'd already chosen. A new outfit never failed to raise a woman's spirits—so she suspected that applied to teenagers, as well. She hoped the teen's mother would be okay. Despite resenting Margo and the impact she'd had on her life, Savannah wouldn't wish her harm.

She indulged herself with a large sundae for lunch, then took her purchases home. She'd arranged for the store to deliver Jacey's dress.

The afternoon stretched out. She thought about Declan. She did laundry. And remembered dancing at the resort in California. Painted her nails and thought about his desire to do the best he could for his daughter. She vacuumed the apartment, even though she and Stacey splurged and had a weekly housekeeper. It helped when they were both gone for up to several weeks at a time. However the mindless activity didn't do anything but offer more opportunities to think about Declan—his dark hair, his eyes gazing into hers, the feel of his mouth on hers.

Calculating the time difference she decided she'd talk to her sister just before bedtime in Spain. She was leaving in another day for Norway; it would be a while before she could talk to Stacey again.

She dialed and waited impatiently for Stacey to answer.

"Hi," she said when she heard her sister's voice. And promptly burst into tears.

"Savannah? What happened? What's wrong?" Stacey's concern came across the line clearly.

"I'm such an idiot."

"As in?"

She heard the concern in her sister's voice.

"My last assignment was with Declan Murdock."

The silence on the line told her how shocked Stacey was.

"Couldn't you have refused?"

"I considered it," Savannah said.

"But?"

"But I went anyway. I still love him."

Stacey's voice was warm with love. "Oh honey, I always wondered. You never found another guy you felt was special. I hoped you'd gotten over him."

"Me, too. Actually, I thought I had. Until I spent the past three weeks with him."

"I take it you aren't seeing him anymore?"

"No. And it's almost the same reason. His wife was injured and he rushed to her side."

"Shall I fly home?" Stacey asked.

Savannah wiped her eyes with the back of her hands. "No. I'm leaving for Norway and would be gone by the time you got here. I just wanted to talk a little."

"I have the rest of the night," Stacey said softly.

Savannah leaned back on the sofa, closed her eyes and told her sister about Declan and Jacey and the time in California. Especially about when she'd realized she loved Declan and how she'd tried to put some distance between them, while spending as much time as she could with him— just for a few memories to cling to down through the years.

As she wound down, she ended with, "He's no more interested in me this time than last time. Why can't I find some darling man who is single, unattached, no baggage and who would love me to distraction?"

"The heart loves whom it loves," Stacey said. "Sometimes the person loves back, sometimes not. Your love is still there, not diminished by his not returning it. I'm so sorry it's bringing you pain instead of happiness. I can relate. I didn't know Luis loved me until he finally proposed. I thought I was going to end up at home nursing a broken heart, so I feel for you, sis."

"At least I only have the next couple of days to get through and then my next assignment takes me to Norway. I'm counting on the country to be as pretty as Alaska."

They spent a few minutes talking about the

coming weeks and tentative plans Stacey and Luis had made.

Savannah hung up feeling marginally better. Her sister had the dilemma of having to fulfill contracts when all she wanted was to stay with Luis. Savannah looked forward to her busy schedule to keep her from dwelling on Declan.

Sunday night her cell rang. Jacey. Savannah almost answered, but decided she didn't need another confrontation the night before she left. She let it go to voice mail—if the girl would even leave a message. She could listen to it when she felt not so fragile.

Finished with her packing, she went to the kitchen to pull out the small container of chocolate-chocolate-chip ice cream. It was her favorite comfort food. The small container was still too much for one person, but she made serious headway through it. Putting the remainder back, she took a shower and went to bed early.

To lie awake for endless hours as she had the past three nights, thinking about Declan, the kisses they'd shared, the discussions they'd had. Trying to remember that the whole adventure had been just an assignment, not the prelude to a long life together.

Savannah met up with the family she'd accompany the next morning at JFK airport, just before boarding the plane to Oslo. Too busy now to think about might-have-beens, she greeted the three children and once on board had them occupied with coloring books and handheld games. For the next two weeks she'd enjoy Norway, make sure her charges were happy and that the parents had a carefree vacation. She did her job well.

And her plan worked—except at night. No matter how tired she was, it was hard to fall asleep. And once asleep, more than once she dreamed of Declan. Some dreams were sweet—he laughed and held her hand. Others had them plunging off cliffs on a mountain trail. She never dreamed about Jacey. But every once in a while when she had a free few minutes, she wondered how Declan was faring with his daughter. Had her mother recovered? Was she still planning to live with him for the next few years? She hoped so. He deserved to be happy. Just because she wasn't the one to make him happy, she still wished him well.

Her heart ached for him. He'd been so happy to see the change in his daughter, so delighted when she'd said she wanted to live with him for the next few years. Savannah hoped that hadn't changed—for both their sakes.

The two weeks ended on a happy note and Savannah gave her charges a hug when they parted at JFK upon their return to the U.S. She'd miss those kids. They had been so enchanted with Norway. She laughed, remembering some of their attempts to speak Norwegian—her own included. Fortunately, all those on whom they'd tried out the language had been friendly and helpful.

She got her luggage, hailed a cab and settled back, glad to be home if only for a couple of days.

She had her cell phone with her, but had stupidly left the charger at the apartment. Not that she could have used it in Norway, it was strictly a U.S. phone, but she'd be able to check in with Stephanie now. Was Stacey home or had she thrown caution to the wind and canceled her assignments to spend more time with Luis and his boys? She didn't think her sister would have backed out of an assignment without someone to take over despite being a woman in love.

She sighed and watched as the familiar scenery sped by. She didn't think she would have forsaken Vacation Nannies instantly if Declan had been more interested in her. But she would have been tempted not to spend a day apart from him. Now they'd spend a lifetime apart.

She didn't know what had happened to him in the past two weeks. She remembered the weeks and months after he'd left before. She didn't want a repeat this time.

When she reached her apartment, she kicked off her shoes and dragged her suitcase into the bedroom. She'd unpack later. Right now she wanted to open windows and air the place out. Being shut up for a couple of weeks in summer made it more than stuffy.

After a slight breeze began to permeate the apartment, she fished out her phone and plugged in the charger. She went to see if there was anything edible in the kitchen or if she needed to do some quick shopping. She wrinkled her nose at the stale bread and over two-week-old eggs. Dumping both, she went to shower and change. Shopping next and then she'd call Stephanie. Saturdays the office manager worked until noon, as some people found it more convenient to come in for interviews on the weekend.

Once showered and dressed, Savannah went to the phone and called the office.

She got an answering machine. Stephanie was probably busy with a client. Grabbing her purse, she headed out. She knew her next assignment wouldn't start before Monday, so had time to herself for at least a day and a half. Which meant—a lunch at her favorite deli and then grocery shopping. Better on a full stomach anyway, she rationalized. She loved Sol's. It was the best deli in the area and always packed. Today was no exception. It was good to be home, and back in her routine.

Slipping the key into her lock a couple of hours later, Savannah was feeling good. She was full, had two bags of fresh fruit and salad fixings, and a new carton of chocolate-chocolate-chip ice cream. Could life get much better?

Just as she finished putting everything away, the phone rang.

"Home safe and sound?" Stephanie said when she answered.

"I am and will have my report on the family in by Monday. I can mail it if I'm leaving right away." They kept records of the childrens' likes and dislikes, favorite toys or games, and other facts that would help the next time around. And so often that made the second or subsequent assignments that much easier on all. "Are you still at the office?"

"No, I'm home, just calling to see that you made it back. I left the Pendergasts' folder on my desk if you go in before Monday. You don't have to meet up with them until four. It's a late flight to Maine. Also, I never got a report on Murdock," Stephanie murmured.

Savannah looked at the ceiling. She didn't want to write Declan up as a client. She felt a pang of longing to see him again. See how he was doing. Find out what had happened between him and his daughter and his ex-wife. Did Jacey get her walking cast?

"I'll include that one, as well," she said as the silence ticked on. She didn't want Stephanie questioning her closely on that assignment.

"Did you have fun in Norway?"

"It was amazing." Savannah told her about the beautiful scenery she'd enjoyed. She had had a good time, despite thinking of Declan all the time.

"Want to have dinner tomorrow night?" Stephanie asked.

"Sure, we can catch up even more. How about Antoine's on Fourth?" Savannah suggested.

"Meet you at seven."

That gave Savannah more than a day to decide what she'd say about Declan and the assignment to California. And to hope she could pass it off as a regular assignment enough to pass Stephanie's alert.

She went to check on her phone. It was fully charged—and there were forty-seven missed calls.

As she thumbed through them, she saw they were all from one phone—Declan's. Her heart jumped. The first bunch were the second day she was gone. Then several each day since then. The last one had been two hours ago.

Why was he calling her?

Almost afraid to find out, she debated returning the calls. Maybe later. She put the phone down and went to unpack. She had enough to do to keep her busy. She didn't need to respond to calls from a one-time client.

But as the afternoon went on she couldn't help obsessing about his calls. What did he want? Was everything okay? How was Jacey doing? Tempting as it was to call him, she resisted. Almost as if testing her resolve.

Savannah was curled up on the sofa watching reruns that evening and eating her favorite ice cream when her phone rang. Hesitating only a moment, she rose and went to answer, already knowing who was on the other end of the line.

"Savannah?" It was Declan.

"Hi."

"You're home now?"

"Yes, I arrived home today." She wished her heart didn't race just hearing his voice. She closed her eyes to better picture him.

"I've been trying for weeks to reach you."

"I only have U.S. service and have been in Europe. I didn't hear any messages."

"No, I, uh, didn't want to leave messages. Are you free?"

"For what?"

"I'd like to see you."

"Why?"

"Because I've missed you?" he said tentatively.

She sure had missed him, but she thought they might put different emphasis on their version of missed.

"It's too late for dinner, I'm sure you've eaten," he said.

She looked at the clock, it was after eight. "I did, and right now I'm enjoying dessert."

"Want to go out for a drink or coffee or something?"

"No, thank you. It's really late in Europe and I'm still on that time zone. I'm going to bed soon."

"Tomorrow for breakfast then?"

Her heart raced. He wanted to see her. She had a million reasons why she should refuse. But— she wanted to see him again.

"I'll pick you up at seven," he said when she didn't respond.

"So no sleeping in for me tomorrow," she murmured, trying to come up with a reason why she should refuse. A reason that wouldn't tell him how foolish she'd been to fall in love with him again.

"Too early?"

"No." She wished she felt up to seeing him to-night. But she was tired and she wanted all her senses fully alert when meeting Declan again.

"See you then."

"Right." She ended the call, wondering what he had meant by *missing* her.

She should have asked about Jacey. Maybe the teen would be at breakfast in the morning.

Finishing what she wanted of the ice cream, she put it away and went to bed. She was tired, but even so, as on every other night for the past two weeks, she didn't fall asleep right away. Her thoughts dwelt on Declan. She would see him in a few short hours. To what end? Nothing had changed.

Not that she cared. At least she'd see him for a little while.

She wore a pretty lavender sundress the next morning and white sandals. Her hair was done to her satisfaction. Her eyes sparkled as she stared at herself in the mirror and counted the minutes until he'd arrive. She hoped—well, she wasn't going to set herself up for disappointment. She'd see what he had to say.

When the knock came at the door, Savannah was ready. She threw it open and stared a moment, surprised by her delight at seeing him. He looked wonderful in a dark shirt, dark slacks and wind-blown hair.

"Ah, ready, I see. You were always prompt."

"I learned that from my business teacher," she said, picking up a small purse and pulling the door closed. He didn't move and for a moment she wondered—then he leaned over to kiss her. His lips were warm and firm and so exciting she almost dropped her purse. Her knees grew wobbly as he kissed her and kissed her. Finally he stood tall and looked into her eyes, his own questioning. "I've been wanting to do that for two weeks."

What could she say? This meeting ranked right up there with the top ten stupid things she'd ever done. They had no future together. She knew that. She'd wanted so much more than a kiss, but couldn't reveal that. Yet she couldn't deny she'd been a willing and active partner in the kisses.

Floundering around for something to say, she grasped on Jacey.

"How's Jacey doing?"

"Getting around like a pro on her walking cast. She doesn't seem at all hampered by it, though she says her ankle itches all the time and she's careful not to get any tan until it comes off."

"Ah, following her mother's advice. And how is Margo?" Not that she really wanted to know. Better to keep reminding herself about the other woman. She was never going away.

"Doing better than the doctors originally expected. She's in a convalescent hospital in Queens."

"Doing all right without your help?" she couldn't resist asking.

"Yes, well, that's another situation. Best saved for later. I thought we could walk to Marney's on the Battery. It's still cool enough to enjoy eating outside. And I hope everyone else in the city wanted to sleep in so we won't have to wait for a table."

They walked the few blocks to Battery Park and followed a pathway to the small café that had a view of the harbor. Declan had his wish, as well—there were several vacant tables. Taking the one with the best view, they soon ordered and settled back, sipping hot coffee. The day would grow hot soon, but right now the temperature was ideal.

"So update me about Jacey," she said.

"She had a hard few days while Margo was still in a coma. Once she woke, she's improved daily. Jacey visits her almost every day. She's still set on moving in with me, however, which was in doubt for a few days. Her mother's dead set against it, so there's a lot of tension there."

"It's the money, isn't it?" she said.

He nodded.

"Putting Jacey right in the middle of it all."

"I know. I don't like it, but she is taking a more pragmatic view of her mother these days. She told me when Margo starts complaining about money, she changes the subject."

"Is Margo any good at what she does—selling high-end fashion?" Savannah asked after a moment. "Surely that should bring in enough money for her."

He shrugged. "To hear her tell it, one day she's leading sales person, the next she's so poor she needs more child support. It's hard to know what's what with her. But she's had the job for several years, so I expect she's doing something right."

Breakfast arrived and the conversation turned away from the Murdock family.

"Tell me about your trip," he invited.

Glad for the safe topic, Savannah told him about the cruise, the gorgeous scenery and the fun she and the children had had. He asked questions which showed his interest. He watched her as she talked, his eyes delving deep into hers. A couple of times Savannah felt flustered by so much attention.

He looked around when she finished.

"It's pretty here, too," he said.

"Of course. New York is home. But I'm glad I got to see the fjords. Reminded me of part of Alaska on my other cruise."

He studied her for a moment. "You love the travel part, don't you?"

"I do. And I'll forever be grateful for learning enough from your course to make Vacation Nannies a success."

He nodded, his face losing expression.

"What?" she asked.

"Nothing." He took a sip of coffee. "Oh, I almost forgot. Jacey told me to be sure and give you this." He fished an envelope out of his pocket and handed it to her. It was yellow and small. She lifted the flap and drew out a thank-you card. Smiling, she opened it and read, "Savannah, thank you for the dress. It's very pretty and I will love wearing it once I can walk again. It's okay if you and my dad see each other. I wish he'd marry someone who would make him happy. If it can't be my mom, I want it to be you."

It was signed with X's and O's and a big *Jacey*.

"A thank you for her dress," she murmured, replacing it in the envelope and tucking it into her purse.

"That was nice of you. She really likes it. Hasn't worn it yet, though."

"She says she will when she can walk again."

"Or when we go someplace where she'd need a dress. We haven't done all that much while she's been hampered by the cast."

His phone rang and he glanced at who was calling, then with a quick, "Excuse me," he answered. "Hi, Jacey, what's up?"

Savannah watched his expression change as his daughter spoke to him. She could tell he was getting angry again, or at least extremely frustrated.

"Tell your mother—never mind, I'll call her myself. Don't worry about it. She and I will discuss the situation."

He hung up and glared at Savannah for a moment, not seeing her. Margo made him so angry he wanted to throw something.

"That was good," she said.

"What?"

"That you are not putting Jacey in the middle of you and Margo. At first I thought you were going to give her a message to relay."

"That would be too easy. I need to get it through her head that Jacey is old enough to decide and she's decided to live with me."

He looked over the river, still seething with Margo's attempted manipulation of their daughter.

"May I make a suggestion?" Savannah said hesitantly.

He wondered what she had to offer in this mess. For a second he hoped she'd offer to watch Jacey until she was better—or for the entire summer.

"If a manager hasn't been hired yet, put her in charge of that little boutique sports store you're putting in the resort in California."

"Have you lost your mind?" he asked. "Why in the world would I have anything more to do with Margo than I need to? I certainly—" He stopped talking and looked at her. She looked as pretty as he remembered. She'd been the smartest, quickest student in the class he'd taught. But how could she think he'd want to work with Margo?

"You're an astute businessman—listen for a minute. You said she's good at selling, or could be. That new shop will be in a high-end resort with tons of luxury items and amenities. Rich people come to stay. She might meet her rich husband there. The pay will probably be excellent. You could arrange for her to live at the resort. And she'd be three thousand miles away from your daughter when you and Jacey need time to get your own family traditions and routines started."

For a moment all he could do was rail against the idea of doing anything to help the woman who had caused such havoc in his life. But slowly his temper cooled and he began to see the merit in what Savannah suggested. He'd have to play around with the idea for a little while, assess the pros and cons, but the more he thought about it, the more he liked the idea. He could have Margo train in the San Francisco office. She'd love that city. Then she could settle in at the resort before the cold weather hit, so she'd see it in the best season.

"She couldn't report directly to me," he murmured.

Savannah smiled slowly. He caught his breath, wanting to reach across the table and kiss her.

"Something to think about," she said.

"It has some merit," he said cautiously.

"I think Jacey will be fine with the idea, knowing her mother's being taken care of. Some of her hesitation in moving in with you was concern for her mother. She's seen the resort, seen San Francisco, so she can picture where her mother's living. Jacey would love visiting her at the resort maybe for the full summer next year."

"Giving me the summer free," he said pensively.

"Did you want that?"

"Maybe, in the future," he said. He looked at

her plate. She was finished. He was finished. Summoning the waiter for the bill, he paid then looked at Savannah. "Want to walk along the water for a while?"

"Sure. I have no plans until tonight."

"What's tonight?" he asked as they rose and wound their way through the other tables. Every one was occupied now.

"I'm meeting a friend for dinner," she said.

Declan felt the words like a blow. He didn't want her seeing anyone else. They'd spent almost three weeks together and she had not mentioned a special man in her life. Yet he'd done nothing to make sure that never happened. Had he left it too late?

He turned toward the right and they walked along the wide asphalt pathway.

"Now or never," he murmured, glancing around. Except for the couple on the rollerblades moving away from them, they were alone on the path.

"Now or never for what?" she asked.

He turned, picking up her hand in his. Hands linked, he looked at her.

Took a breath.

"Savannah Williams, will you marry me?"

She stared at him dumbfounded.

"The thought of you going out with someone else is driving me nuts. I was going to wait for the perfect setting. See you a few more times. Take you for dinner, dancing. Have you see I'm not the man I was seven years ago? I want you to trust me. I want you to want me as much as I want you. I let you down, I know I did, and you suffered the most for my stupid decision seven years ago. I thought I was doing the right thing. It turned out to be a disaster. For all of us, but most of all for you."

She nodded slowly. He couldn't read her expression.

"Say something."

"I'm thinking," she replied.

Declan frowned. "About?"

"There's so much to consider. Jacey, Margo. I want—well I wanted this seven years ago. Instead you walked away without a backward look. You'll never know how much that hurt."

The pain in her eyes told him. "It wasn't without a backward look, or regrets. I hardly had the marriage vows out of my mouth before I knew it was a mistake. I tried—I really tried, for both Jacey's sake and yours."

"Mine?" Savannah said in surprise.

"I knew I had hurt you badly. It couldn't have been in vain. I had to make a go of the marriage or I would have to face the fact I threw away the best thing I'd ever had for nothing. And that was too hard to accept."

"We're not the same people," she said slowly, her eyes seeking his, searching for…what?

"No. I hope I'm a better man. You are still the bright young woman who gave me such joy. If you can find it in you to forgive me, I will spend the rest of my life making up for that hurt."

"What if you change your mind again?" she asked tentatively.

He felt her words like a slap. Yet how could he blame her?

"I won't. I didn't even years ago—I just pushed you away to do my duty. I found it wasn't enough. I didn't seek you out when the divorce was final. I didn't try to regain our trust or love then. But I thought about you every day. Much as I hated the way Jacey was behaving, I saw it as a way to have you back in my life. To see how you were, if there was anything there for you and me."

"It was a ploy?" she asked.

"No. A gift. I looked at it as a miracle—your taking the assignment. The more I was around you the more my love strengthened. I've loved you for eight years. With you or without you, I'll always love you, Savannah. I just hope it'll be with you."

"Why? Why are you asking me and why now?"

"Why? Because we're meant to be together. I knew that seven years ago. I hurt you. I'm so sorry. I didn't feel good myself or about myself when I left the café that night. But I was focused on the daughter I'd never known I had."

Savannah watched his eyes carefully

"I honestly thought I was doing the best thing for her. It wasn't until a few days later I realized how much doing that would end up costing me. Margo is nothing like you. I loved you. I should have married you on the spot and dealt with Jacey in another fashion."

Savannah tilted her head slightly. "As in?"

"Gotten custody, introduced her to you. She

was adorable at seven. You two would have hit it off."

"Yet when Margo was hurt you rushed to her side," Savannah said slowly. Her heart beat so fast she could hardly think.

"I rushed her daughter to her side—there's a difference. I don't blame you for not trusting me. I don't know how to build trust back except to ask you to give me a chance. I swear you'll never regret it."

Savannah pulled her hand from his and turned slightly. "I have to think about this," she said.

"Look at the weeks we spent together. Everything meshed. You enjoyed the hiking as I did. Never complained. At the resort you introduced Jacey to all those amenities as if you were born to them. You talk as well with businessmen as their wives. You don't mind getting dirty. And you clean up really good." He wasn't going to talk about their kisses, the touches that drove him crazy, the yearning and desire and everything else that he felt around her.

She shook her head. "Those are not reasons to get married."

Declan felt a wave of panic. He'd asked her and

she was going to say no. He'd apologized for his thoughtless rejection years ago. He'd promised to do better. He thought they'd rediscovered each other in California. He would have asked her the day she came for the interview when he realized his feelings were as strong as ever. But he needed some hint from her that she returned his feelings. Only Margo's accident and Savannah's next assignment had delayed the proposal.

Now he couldn't imagine going through the years ahead alone. Savannah had shown him what a real family could be like. And he wanted it—with her.

He floundered around for something else to offer. "Jacey would love to have you for a stepmother."

"I wouldn't be marrying Jacey," she said.

"You're not making this easy," he said with a frown.

She looked back at him, her expression impossible to read.

"I love you, Savannah. I have for years. Even when I was exchanging vows with Margo, determined to make that second marriage work for Jacey's sake, I almost stopped, knowing it wasn't her I loved but you. I can't imagine my life without you. It would be dead and empty. It's already been dead and empty for seven years. Please, join your life with mine and let me cherish and love you the rest of our lives."

She laughed and flung herself against him, hugging him tightly. "You love me? You've always loved me?" she asked, then kissed him as if there was no tomorrow.

He didn't question her reaction, just kissed her with all the years of pent-up love. If they lived to be a hundred, it would never be enough time to make up to her for the lost years.

People walked by, he didn't care. He'd kiss her until dark if she'd let him.

She pushed back a fraction and opened her blue eyes, gazing up into his. "My answer is yes, in case you were still wondering."

"I had hoped that with the kiss. But for a few moments, I wasn't sure." His heart raced with her response. "How soon before we can get married?"

"Months yet. I have assignments to fulfill. My sister to marry off. And a future to plan. Plus you'll need that time to cement the bond with

Jacey so she doesn't feel threatened when we get married."

"I love you. I don't know if I can wait months. We have lost time to make up."

"Yes, you can wait. Did I mention I love you, too? Declan, I have since before you left me that night in that café. I've never been back. I tried so hard to get over you. And I even convinced myself I had when you interviewed me. But that was so bogus. I first fell in love with you at your class, and I never did get over it."

He hugged her tightly. "I am so sorry we wasted the years."

"You did what you thought best. Even though I hated it, I understood it. I'm sorry for your sake it didn't work."

"I never loved Margo, not then, certainly not now. Everything I did was for Jacey. And rushing to the hospital was the right thing to do for my daughter."

"It felt like the past all over again. Margo before me."

"I'd figured that out by the time we left the hospital," he said, brushing his lips against hers again. "I should have gone after you right then.

But Jacey needed me. The thing is, Savannah, she might need me a lot in the next few years."

"I've never resented Jacey. It was only Margo."

"You never had competition there."

"It didn't seem like it when you married her!" she said.

He grimaced. "I will never marry again unless it's you and only you. I plan for it to be forever. My dad and mom were happy up to the day she died. That's what I want for us. And for Jacey when she gets married. Let's show her how a great marriage works."

"I'd love to be part of that project," Savannah said, reaching up to kiss him again. "I love you, Declan. I always have, and I believe I always will."

"I'm counting on it," he said, kissing her again. The future was theirs. He didn't know why he got her forgiveness, only that Savannah was the most loving person he knew. And she loved him. Together they'd forge a loving and happy partnership that would last a lifetime.

\* \* \* \* \*

*Mills & Boon® Large Print*

*September 2012*

**A VOW OF OBLIGATION**
Lynne Graham

**DEFYING DRAKON**
Carole Mortimer

**PLAYING THE GREEK'S GAME**
Sharon Kendrick

**ONE NIGHT IN PARADISE**
Maisey Yates

**VALTIERI'S BRIDE**
Caroline Anderson

**THE NANNY WHO KISSED HER BOSS**
Barbara McMahon

**FALLING FOR MR MYSTERIOUS**
Barbara Hannay

**THE LAST WOMAN HE'D EVER DATE**
Liz Fielding

**HIS MAJESTY'S MISTAKE**
Jane Porter

**DUTY AND THE BEAST**
Trish Morey

**THE DARKEST OF SECRETS**
Kate Hewitt

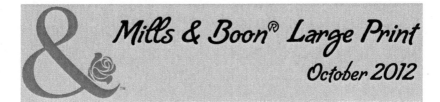

*Mills & Boon® Large Print*
*October 2012*

## A SECRET DISGRACE
Penny Jordan

## THE DARK SIDE OF DESIRE
Julia James

## THE FORBIDDEN FERRARA
Sarah Morgan

## THE TRUTH BEHIND HIS TOUCH
Cathy Williams

## PLAIN JANE IN THE SPOTLIGHT
Lucy Gordon

## BATTLE FOR THE SOLDIER'S HEART
Cara Colter

## THE NAVY SEAL'S BRIDE
Soraya Lane

## MY GREEK ISLAND FLING
Nina Harrington

## ENEMIES AT THE ALTAR
Melanie Milburne

## IN THE ITALIAN'S SIGHTS
Helen Brooks

## IN DEFIANCE OF DUTY
Caitlin Crews